Scream, Queen!

STEPHANIE SPARKS

For Ken

Scream, Queen!

Chapter 1

*A*s Becca St. James walked the long, dusty unpaved road to school, the old grain elevator peeking up from the trees beyond the road, she gripped her backpack straps and wondered what the first day of class would bring.

She almost didn't notice the speeding car bearing down on her.

She was lost in her head, thinking about how the summer's heat had leaked into the start of the school year, and it had been so hot these past few months that if you could pinch Morganville between your fingers and blow, the arid little town would wisp away. Some days, when she allowed herself to daydream, she imagined being one of those wisps, like the fluff of a dandelion, floating off to

7

bigger, better places.

Like college and then med school.

The car's loud, rumbling engine pulled her out of her thoughts as it flew toward her in a cloud of dust. A black muscle car with tinted windows, gold-painted bumper, and a fierce bird emblazoned on its shiny hood. *Won't be shiny for long,* she thought, *not the way this maniac drives.*

She rushed to the side of the road, ready to dive into the ditch if the driver swerved toward her. Her white sneakers kicked through the mud, and while she feared getting hit, she was upset that her brand new outfit was going to look lousy before she even got to school.

The car screeched to a stop, spraying rocks and grit. As the dust settled, the driver leaned across the passenger seat and cranked down the window.

"Becs, look!" It was Travis Valcourt, grinning like a wild child. His black hair was slicked back, and his green eyes shined. Butterflies fluttered in her stomach at the sight of his boyish grin and his perfect teeth.

Her grandmother called him Becca's "handsome fella," since he started hanging around early in the summer while she worked at the local burger joint. And then he asked her out on a couple of dates. They had been together ever since, and yet his attention to her still made her blush.

"Look what my dad got me!"

Becca wasn't big into cars. She knew she wanted one — needed one — if she was ever going to get out of town.

But whereas Travis had well-off parents that could afford to give him a fancy car and new clothes, Becca had to scrimp and save all her money just to buy a brand new pair of sneakers that were now ruined. Still, she could appreciate his excitement.

"So cool," she said, peering inside.

"It's an '84 Firebird," he said beaming. "Burt Reynolds has one just like her!"

"Wow. What for?"

"What do ya mean 'what for?' It's the first day of the last year of high school — a guy needs a car. I've been begging my dad for months! And finally!"

"Congratulations," she said, genuinely happy for him.

"Oh, no," he said, curling his finger in a motion to get her inside. "Congrats to *us*. You're never going to have to walk anywhere again."

"Really?" Now she was interested. Morganville was a safe town. The crime rate was low (mainly because there weren't many people left to stir up too much trouble), but anytime Becca had to go to the library on main street, she had to convince Travis or one of her classmates to go with her all because of the creepy homeless guy that slept on the benches near there. He mostly left people alone, but anytime Becca saw him, he would stare her down.

When she told Gran about it, Gran just warned her from getting too close. "He's trouble."

Travis patted the passenger seat. "Jump in."

His handsome grin put a smile on her face and after taking off her backpack, she crouched down to get inside.

He reached around her shoulders and pulled her in close. "Missed you."

She laughed. "You saw me two days ago."

"So?"

She leaned in, catching a whiff of his aftershave. Travis was the first guy in school to start shaving — in seventh grade. He was also the only one who looked like a man, and that was just what Becca appreciated about him. He was grown up and so was she. She was ready to make adult decisions about her future — and other stuff.

She looked down at her hands folded in her lap. Travis pinched her chin between his thumb and forefinger, forcing her gaze back to him. "Kiss me," he said.

Those damn butterflies turned her insides into jelly. When they parted and he put the car in gear, she wanted to reach out and stop him. Climb into his lap and—

The car jerked forward, picking up speed. Becca grabbed the door handle. Travis reached over and took her other hand, with his forearm steering the wheel. None of it was safe, but Becca was starting to tire of playing it safe. She was tired of being a good, little high school girl. She was going to university next year. She was going to be an adult, so it was time to start acting like one.

She squeezed Travis's hand between her legs and smiled shyly.

* * *

The first day was always a mad rush, but Becca was prepared. She had picked up her textbooks the week before and took the time to wander around to double check the location of her locker and all her classrooms. So she spent her morning getting Travis and his friends oriented.

Travis hooked his arm around her neck and kissed the top of her head. "Told ya she's perfect," he bragged.

Chester Miller, Heath Cowlie, and Mark Peters shrugged in agreement. They were all big guys: Chester played football; Heath played track and field, and had just signed up to be one of the town's volunteer firefighters; and Mark worked on his family's farm all year round. They were good guys too, though Mark used to tease Becca in grade school about being a nerdy bookworm, but he seemed to have forgotten he was once her biggest bully.

Their girlfriends were all pretty and fairly nice. Erin went with Chester, Candace went with Heath, and Mark's girlfriend had dumped him last week, so he spent the precious few moments before the first bell glaring at the poor girl across the indoor courtyard.

Becca grinned at Travis, glad that she wasn't dating a thick-headed farm boy whose idea of romance was probably a literal roll in the hay.

Travis grinned back at her. "You're all smiles today. Don't tell me you're happy to be back to this dump."

Becca loved school, and she would hardly call it a dump. She was happy to be back at school; she liked the routine of seeing familiar faces every day.

But actually, she had been smiling because she had been having adult thoughts — specifically about having sex with Travis.

Erin nudged her with an elbow. "She probably heard the news."

Caught off guard, Becca blushed. "Uh, what news?"

"Trav's dad announced there's gonna be a big festival," she said. She stood too close to Becca, who could smell the girl's combination of cinnamon gum and strawberry lip balm. "Party time."

"Harvest Festival," Chester jumped in, anything to sound like he knew something.

"It's just a stupid town thing," Travis said.

"To *you*, maybe," said Candace. "But someone's gotta be the Harvest Queen."

The PA system crackled over their heads. Most students ignored the sound of the principal's announcements or tried to talk over his voice, but Becca straightened up and strained to hear.

"Becca St. James to the office please. Becca St. James."

The group of friends made an accusing "oooOOOooo" sound and pointed at her.

"What did you do?" teased Candace.

Travis held her hand. "Want me to go with you?"

And do what? Beat up the principal? Aggression was Travis's primary response to any situation in which he was at a disadvantage.

She patted his arm and smiled. "It's probably fine. I'll

catch you later?"

He squeezed her hand and kissed it. "Yeah. Later."

She hurried through the busy halls and into the even busier office, where the admin staff coordinated with overwhelmed students who didn't know how to read their schedules nor wanted to be there.

She found Principal MacMillan in his stuffy office, sitting across from a student she had never seen before.

The new guy wore an olive-green army jacket and gray high-tops. Or maybe they had once been white, like her own muddied sneakers.

He was cute, if a little geeky. If he traded in his round-framed glasses for contact lenses and ran a brush or some gel through his shaggy hair, he would almost give Travis a run for his money.

"Miss St. James, I suppose you know why you're here?" said the principal.

"I don't, sir."

"This is James Martin," he explained. "He's starting here today, and since you're on the Welcome Committee, I expect you'll show him around and help him get settled."

Becca froze. She had the vaguest memory of signing up to volunteer for the Welcome Committee when she first started at Morganville High. She already had her sights set on med school and knew that she was going to need to build up her volunteer experience, but in the years since, she hadn't done any work with the committee.

Becca had selfishly kept the position on her resume because she figured it was so minor that she could fake her way through it if anyone asked her about it.

But today, at a moment when she needed to fake it, she wasn't sure she was up to the task. She swallowed, shifting in her seat. "Mr. MacMillan, I—"

"I knew you were the person to ask," he said. "Now go on. Show Mr. Martin the ropes."

Becca stood up. She and the new kid bumped into each other as they tried to squeeze out of the small office at the same time. James invited her to exit first, and she quickly threw her backpack over her shoulder and scurried out.

They left the busy office and stood in the hallway, where James held out a hand. Becca stared at it until she realized he wanted to shake hers. He smiled when she finally did. "We, uh, have the same name."

She stared blankly. "Oh?"

He pointed to himself. "James. And you're *St.* James."

"Oh, yeah. Weird." She laughed politely, then stopped to clear the warble out of her throat. *Come on, get it together*, she told herself. *You have a job to do. Help the new guy feel welcome.* "Do you have your class schedule?" She held out a hand to take it from him as he pulled a folded sheet of paper from his breast pocket.

"Sure do."

"Great." She scanned it over. "Okay, so— Oh, boy. You've got Mr. Walsh for math first thing? You're going to want to be there before the bell rings because—"

"Have we met before?" he asked.

"Umm, I don't think so…"

"Huh," he said. "I could've sworn we've met."

She handed the schedule back. "I guess I just have one of those faces."

He tucked the schedule back in his pocket as she began to delve into the ins and outs of the school. He cut her off. "Look, it's real nice of you to want to help me out, but I don't need a tour guide," James said. "Just tell me where the library is so I can check out some books."

Library? He reads books? James already wasn't like other guys she knew.

"Sure, it's that way on your right," she said, pointing down the hall.

He nodded in thanks and headed off in that direction. As he hoisted his backpack on his shoulder, a few pieces of paper fluttered down from an unzipped pocket. Becca raced to pick them up before other students stepped all over it.

"Wait!" she called out, holding the papers out to him. He had turned the corner and was gone.

"Shoot," she muttered. She made a neat pile of what looked like scribbled notes and photocopies of old news articles.

One featured a photo of her mom, Bethany St. James, from the year she had died. Her mother's frozen, grainy face stared into oblivion.

What is the new guy doing with this?

Chapter 2

"**S**o here's the thing," said Erin, between long sips of her Grape Crush. "You have to be nominated by someone on town council. No exceptions."

Becca had her head down, staring at James's notes and the photo of her mom in her lap when Travis set a lunch tray in front of her. She startled and he gave her a wink. "My treat." He tore a chunk out of his apple and addressed the table of friends. "Whatcha talkin' about?"

"*Harvest Queen,*" Erin replied. "It's all everyone's been talking about."

"It's all *you've* been talking about," said Candace, throwing her balled-up straw wrapper at Erin's forehead. "No one's gonna nominate you anyway."

She put an arm around Travis, who straightened in

mock surprise. "My dearest friend Trav will. His daddy is the reeve."

"That sounds like an abuse of power," he said.

"Nepotism," Becca chimed in. The others stared at her, making her blush. She looked back down again. *I should have kept my mouth shut. Why do I always have to be such a know-it-all?*

Travis sloughed off Erin's arm. "If I'm sucking up to my dad for any of you, it's gonna be for Becca."

The table exploded with different exclamations of *Becca?* and *Harvest Queen?* and even Becca squeaked, "Me?"

Travis spoke only to her, ignoring the curious looks of everyone at the long table. "Yeah, you. You're a knock-out. You'd win for sure." He kissed her hand, making her blush even harder. "And you're already *my* queen."

Erin shrugged. "There's a scholarship on the line too, I guess. But you also get a free gown!"

"Scholarship?" Becca perked up.

As she dared to look around the table, she noticed James Martin pass by, holding a sack lunch. "Oh, hey, James!" she called. The table fell silent as they looked to see who she was yelling at.

James paused. "Hi."

Becca jumped up clumsily. "This fell out of your bag earlier. Sorry I couldn't get it to you sooner." She handed the papers back.

He folded them up and stuffed them into his back pocket. "Thanks."

"Do you want to sit with us?" she asked.

"Who's this?" asked Travis.

Becca blushed. All eyes were on her now. "Sorry. Everyone, this is James Martin. He's new and it's his first day."

"It's *everyone's* first day," Candace corrected, and Becca wished someone would throw a straw wrapper at *her* bitchy face.

"Well, James is from somewhere else," she said. Was he though? He could have been one of those weird home-schooled kids everyone joked about. "You're from somewhere, right?"

James remained standing. "That's right. Edgarton."

"City boy!" hollered Mark and Heath.

Their booming voices startled James, who shrank into his oversized coat like a turtle.

"What brought you here?" Travis asked. He slid an arm around Becca's waist, beckoning her to sit down.

James looked longingly toward the exit. "A car."

The group sat silently.

"Funny," said Travis, in that way that said something was definitely not funny. "You must've been the joker at your old school."

Glancing at Becca's amused face, James stood a little straighter and puffed out his chest. "Not the Joker. Batman, maybe."

Becca bit down on a smile, rubbing Travis's back. She could feel his muscles tense.

He leaned over, whispering in her ear. "Can you

believe this guy? Thinks he's hot shit."

"Give him a break," she whispered back. "He's new."

"Yeah," Travis replied, speaking loud enough for the whole table to hear. "He doesn't get it."

"Excuse me," James said, heading for the door.

"Wait." Becca popped up again. Both James and Travis looked at her in surprise. "Library, right?"

"What?" asked Travis.

"I should show James where the library is," she said. James was about to point out that she had given him directions earlier, when she cut him off. "I'll take you there myself. Be right back."

Travis grabbed her arm, pulling her back down, and laid a long kiss on her lips. The others at the table ooh'd and aww'd. "Don't be long," he said as they parted. Face burning, Becca grabbed her bag and hurried out of the cafeteria with James in tow.

"Your boyfriend, I presume?" James asked when they were away from the cafeteria.

"Travis? Oh, yeah. He's great."

"I'm sure," he said, dryly. "Look, you really don't have to take me."

"I don't mind… And I wanted to ask you something…"

"What's that?"

"The notes you dropped… I don't mean to pry—"

He raised an eyebrow. "You looked at them?"

"Well, not exactly, but you have a picture of my mom in there."

"Oh."

He pulled the notes out and skimmed through them, looking. He spotted the photo right away — she looked spot-on like Becca. He smiled shyly, face reddening. "Ah, that's why you looked so familiar."

"Why do you have it?"

"It's kind of a long story."

"I like long stories," she said, as they stopped outside the library.

He sighed, figuring that he wasn't going to escape without an explanation. "So… okay. I don't want to sound like an asshole, but I'm really not interested in stepping out of my comfort zone or making friends or any of that crap — no offense. It's just that I didn't want to move here and I sure as hell don't want to start over at a new school, not in my final year, so long story short, I'm working on an extra credit report so I can graduate by Christmas."

"Sounds like a lot of work."

"It is," he said. "And what my history teacher told me was that I could turn in something about the town's history. I think *she* thinks that learning about this place is gonna make me want to extend my stay. So anyway, I chose to write this really boring report about Morganville, from past to present."

"And my mom is in there because…?"

He shrugged. "I don't know. I haven't gotten that far. Something to do with some old festival, I think."

Travis came up from behind and put an arm around her shoulders. "Missed you," he said, nuzzling her hair.

"I was coming right back," she said.

"Hey, man," he said to James. "Sorry about back there. I didn't know what your deal was and we don't get a lot of new guys around here."

"No problem." James shifted toward the library.

"Sit with us anytime," said Travis. He snapped his fingers. "You know what? My buddy is throwing a party on Saturday. You should come."

"Uh, I'll think about it."

"Just ask Becca for directions."

James skittishly glanced at her. "Yeah, sure. I'll see." Then he hurried into the library like it was his sanctuary from the possibility of making friends.

"Weird guy, huh?" said Travis.

* * *

I don't think he's that *weird,* Becca thought as she scrubbed and bleached her shoes in the kitchen sink that night. While a pot of coffee brewed, she had laid out her homework on the table alongside her weekly planner that she had filled in to prepare for the term. All her high-lighters were lined up and ready to go.

It was the perfect study environment.

But she kept thinking about James and how lonely it must be to be the only new kid in town. It got her thinking about how she felt sometimes, even though she had been dating Travis all summer and hanging out with his friends, and now they were holding hands in the hallways and sneaking kisses in between classes — and then she realized she had wasted an hour daydreaming about boys.

She decided she had better put her pent-up energy to good use and clean her shoes. The bleach smell was distracting, but so was the thought that James probably had his nose stuck in a book and was working on his extra credit project. *Why hadn't I thought of that?*

But it was too late to start a project like that now. She would have to come up with some other way to pay for college.

Like a scholarship for being the Harvest Queen.

She rolled her eyes. *No, that's stupid. It can't be that much anyway. Gran always says the town's always pinching pennies.*

But when it comes to post-secondary funds, every little bit helps.

She looked over at the beige, slim-line phone on the wall. All she had to do was let Travis know she was interested. He could talk to his dad for her. If his dad said no, then it was a no. She wouldn't ever have to wonder *what if?*

Dropping her shoes in the sink, she went to the phone and dialed Travis's number, hoping Erin and Candace hadn't put their names in first.

Travis's mother picked up.

"Hi, Mrs. Valcourt. I know it's late, but is Travis free? I just have a quick question for him."

"Of course, Becca," said Mrs. Valcourt. "It's so nice to hear from you. We'll have to have you over for another BBQ before the weather goes south. Let me see if Travis is home. One second."

Becca waited, wrapping the cord around her fingers.

There was a click and a pause. Becca's heart thundered in her ears and her face burned. *This is so stupid. I don't really want to be Harvest Queen, do I? I mean, I probably won't win anyway. I'm just going to embarrass myself. No one's going to think I'm pretty enough. I should just hang up and—*

"Hey," Travis crooned into her ear.

Her knees weakened. She gripped the phone. "Uh, hi."

"What's up?"

"Oh, nothing." *Liar! Tell him why you're calling!* "I just, uh…"

"Something the matter?"

"No, uh…" *Spit it out!* "I wanna be queen!" *Idiot.*

"Huh?"

"Sorry, I'm tired. Do you think your dad will nominate me for Harvest Queen? I just thought it would be a really good opportunity to—"

Travis cut her off. "He's right here. Hang on... Dad?"

Oh, no…

All of Becca's brain functions froze as Declan Valcourt got on the line. "Hello?"

She could hardly make a squeak. *Why couldn't Travis just pass the word along?*

Mr. Valcourt was an intimidating man. He was in his mid-forties with a streak of white in his black hair and piercing blue eyes. He had always been very cordial whenever Travis brought Becca to the house, but sometimes it felt like he stared too long, like he was picking her apart.

"Uh, hi, Mr. Valcourt."

"Please, call me Declan. Everyone does."

"Uh, sure." But she physically couldn't say his name. She had been raised to address adults as Mr./Mrs./Ms. Even over the summer when he repeatedly asked her to use his first name, *Declan* sounded unusual and clumsy coming off her tongue.

On top of him being her boyfriend's eagle-eyed father, he was also Morganville's reeve for three terms and counting.

"Travis says you have a question?" he prodded.

"Yes, sir." Her voice wavered as she tried to find her strength. No one ever got what they wanted by *not* asking for it. "I was wondering if you would consider nominating me for Harvest Queen?"

"I'm surprised," he said. "I wouldn't have pegged you for it."

Her face burned. Of course she wasn't good enough. She wasn't as pretty as Candace or as enthusiastic as Erin. She just wasn't Harvest Queen material.

"That's okay," she said, about to hang up. "Sorry to bother you."

"Hold on, I didn't say no," said Mr. Valcourt. "I would love to nominate you. I think you would make a fine Harvest Queen."

Chapter 3

*B*ecca floated on cloud nine for the rest of the week. Travis even brought her flowers the next day at school and started a chant of "all hail the queen!" and Mrs. Winston had to chase him out with threats of detention.

By Saturday, she was coming down off the high because something else was on her mind. Tonight was going to be *the night*. She had brushed up on her sex ed notes and dug out a couple of copies of *Cosmopolitan* that her grandmother thought she had hidden away. She poured over what little information she had as if having sex for the first time was like writing an exam.

"Becca! Your date is here!" called Gran. When Dorothy St. James wasn't able to remember Travis's name, she would call him something else. *Your date.*

Your handsome fella. Your young man. They tried to pretend she was just teasing, but the truth was Gran's dementia was rapidly getting worse. Becca didn't know how to help except to keep taking her to the specialist as regularly as possible, even though the long drive to the city exhausted the old woman and ate up chunks of Becca's studying time. But she couldn't abandon the woman who had taken care of her and raised her.

She also couldn't talk to her about sex. She knew in her heart that her grandmother liked Travis a lot and if they had ever been able to have an honest conversation about sexual health, she probably would have given Becca the thumbs up. But Becca didn't want to burden her grandmother with such thinking.

Maybe if her mom had still been around… Becca opened one of the books on her nightstand. The photo bookmarking her page was that of a striking young woman with long, dark brown hair (like Becca's) and long, willowy limbs. She had a hand up to shield her eyes and wore a wicked grin. The back of the photo said summer 1966. It was taken less than a year before she died.

I'm gonna do it, Mom. I hope you won't be mad. Because that would be terribly hypocritical. Bethany St. James got pregnant and gave birth to her only child before she died of leukemia at nineteen, and aside from the photo she used as a bookmark, she didn't have one single memory of her mother. Just the hollow ache of missing a woman she never knew.

"Becca!" Gran called again.

Becca closed the book and shoved it in a drawer. *I don't need anyone's permission or approval. I am in control of my body.*

Downstairs, Travis stood in the doorway making small talk with Gran and her friend, Sadie. They were yakking his ear off about the puzzle they were going to start tonight. He smiled and nodded, but when he saw Becca, he grabbed his chest and made like he was having a heart attack. Becca stopped halfway down the stairs to give him an exasperated, yet flattered look.

"You look amazing," he said.

And she did. She spent all afternoon picking out what she was going to wear and going through those issues of *Cosmo* to figure out how to fix her hair and makeup, topics she knew hardly anything about. Still, she managed to wow Travis and that was enough.

He held out his elbow. "You ready, my queen?"

Slipping her arm through his, she smiled and nodded. *More than you know.*

* * *

Heath Cowlie had been throwing raging back-to-school parties since the end of junior high, and this was his final year to throw one. He stole the keys to his parents' cabin just outside of town on Pigeon Lake. It was the off season anyway, and no one was going to rat them out. Half of the senior class showed up and crowded into the living room and kitchen, and at some point Becca realized that James wasn't there.

As if reading her mind, Travis asked, "So where's the new guy? Too good for us?"

"I don't know," she said, momentarily distracted from the fluttering in her stomach. "I doubt this is his thing."

"Yeah, you're probably right. Seems way too nerdy for fun." Before Becca could point out that she had been way too nerdy for parties up until she caught Travis's eye, he was yelling across the living room at Mark and Chester to get him a beer.

Becca rubbed her arms, feeling cold when Travis' heat left her, and scurried over to join Candace and Erin by the fireplace. Tommy Lemieux was crumpling up way too many old newspapers and stuffing them into the growing fire. Candace sneered at him.

"Will you believe they'd let anyone come?"

"It's our final year," said Erin. "Let the little spaz have his fun."

"Have either of you seen James Martin?" asked Becca.

"The new kid?" Candace asked. "Why would *he* come?"

"Because I invited him," she replied.

"So? Doesn't mean he's welcome," Candace shot back. "It's not really his scene."

"What does that mean?"

Candace rolled her eyes like it was so obvious. "He hasn't been here all this time. Not like us. He can't just swoop in and enjoy everything we've all worked for."

"Yeah," agreed Erin, sipping on a wine cooler.

Becca frowned at them. "How can you say that? He's worked his way through school like the rest of us."

"Because," was Candace's witty response.

Becca left it at that, and as Candace and Erin picked up the threads of a new conversation, she was about to slip away to find Travis, when they roped her back in.

"I heard you got Mr. Valcourt's nomination," said Erin. "I was kinda hoping…"

Becca tried to make herself small enough to disappear. Erin did say she wanted to be queen and that Travis could have helped her. "Sorry," she said. "I didn't mean to…"

"Whatever," said Erin with a shrug. "What am I gonna do with a scholarship anyway? Chester and I are getting married after grad, so whatever."

"You could still go to college if you wanted to," said Becca. "You might find something you like."

"I don't know. I guess I just like having sex and getting drunk?" She elbowed Becca with a wink. "Know what I'm saying?"

Becca turned beet red because at that moment Travis had come to take her away. "Ladies," he said.

She grabbed his wrist (each of his hands held a beer) and said, "Hey, can we talk?" And before he could answer, she led him outside.

* * *

Becca grit her teeth. Travis's hand, splayed out next to her head, snagged on her hair. Her scalp shrieked, and the sting took her out of the moment. But she persisted. *The first time isn't supposed to be perfect*, she reminded herself.

Travis was on top of her, balancing on one hand while his other fumbled under her shirt and bra. Their mouths mashed together, his tongue prodding hers.

They had found a quiet spot on the beach where Travis laid out a blanket. Before he could ask what she wanted to talk about, she crawled into his arms and started kissing him. Then he laid her down on the blanket, so she could wrap her denim-clad legs around his. They rubbed against each other under the starry sky, breaking apart for air.

Travis's hand eventually found its way to her zipper. He slid it down and squeezed his hand inside her jeans. He used his other hand to balance himself, getting her hair caught in between his fingers.

"Travis?" She tapped his shoulder.

"What, baby?" He only ever called her "baby" when they made out, and he said it in a hushed, sexy tone that set her hormones on fire.

"I-I think I want to do it," she whispered.

He grinned. "You wanna have sex?"

She nodded, feeling like a child asking for permission. She felt herself shrinking.

He leaned back, scrutinizing her in the darkness. "I don't know if you're *actually* ready," he said. "I don't want to rush you into something. Losing your virginity is a big deal to girls."

"It doesn't have to be," she said. She wanted to add

that virginity was just a social construct, and she couldn't "lose" something that didn't actually exist, nor was her worth as a person tied to this imaginary commodity. But she was buzzing with a mix of horniness and shame, and couldn't process a thoughtful argument that would convince him other than, *Take me now!*

He rolled aside, shaking his head. "You're cute."

She sat up. Shame turning to anger. "What does that mean?"

"It means you're not ready."

"Says who? You had sex when you were fifteen!"

"Yeah, but I was mature for my age. And besides, I want it to be special for you."

She held his hand. "It'll be special if we're together."

"But on a beach at Heath's parents' lake house? Naw, that's not special."

Her shoulders slumped, and she sighed as she zipped up and adjusted her shirt. Utter disappointment wasn't how she imagined this night. *At least I didn't get knocked up.*

"I'll make sure, when the time is right, that it'll be special for you," he said. "For both of us. Okay?"

She didn't want to fight with Travis. Not over this and not at this moment. They had never had an argument before. Sure, he sometimes said the wrong thing or vocalized an unpopular opinion to test people, and she never called him out on it. Tonight, however—

He's being stupid. She crossed her arms, pouting. *But maybe he is right. Maybe I'm not ready. I'm acting like a bratty kid.*

He cocked his head toward the party. "Wanna go back in?"

A cold breeze blew in off the lake. Becca rubbed her arms. "I think I'd rather go home."

He sighed. At least they were both frustrated. "It's only midnight…"

"I want to go home," she repeated.

"Maybe I *should've* just banged ya, then I could go get my drink on," he grumbled.

She bristled. They stared at each other for a beat before she jumped up, brushing sand off her jeans. "Forget it."

"Hey," he said, scratching the back of his head. "You know I didn't mean it. I was just spouting off."

As she stormed off to beg Erin to take her home, Travis fumbled after her. He didn't give chase or offer a sincere apology. His words washed over her like water, until one sentiment hit its mark.

"You're not going to win Harvest Queen with that attitude!"

Chapter 4

*J*ames Martin had his head stuck in a book, scribbling notes. He spent half his weekend at the public library and the other half at home reading a few books he had checked out about the history of Morganville.

As boring as the research was, he was committed to his "get out of jail early" plan, even if that meant leaving his mom behind so he could move back to the city. And even if he couldn't move away by Christmastime, he would at least get his diploma early so he wouldn't have to go back to school in January. He could hang around for a few months, or maybe apply for early admission to college. But there was no way in hell he was staying at Morganville High any longer than necessary.

HIGH SCHOOL HELL, he wrote in his notebook.

He flipped the page of the *Morganville News*, a 1966 edition from an archive of yellowed old papers that the high school library kept around. He wasn't sure what he was looking for — some odd piece of trivia about the town's history — but he wasn't expecting to see *her* again.

Becca St. James.

There she was, clear as day, in a row of old yearbook photos of other pretty girls with their hair done up in bouffant styles. Becca — no, it was her mom, *Bethany* — had hers flat-ironed straight. While the girl in the picture was as beautiful and fresh-faced as his new classmate, Bethany had a mischievous smirk on her lips.

James swallowed nervously. Did he think Becca was beautiful? That was an odd thing to think about a girl he just met, but he had been thinking about her a lot — and gazing a bit too long at the clipping of her mom.

"Hi, James." Becca interrupted his daydream, pointing to the chair across from him. "Mind if I sit here? I know you're busy, so I won't make a peep."

Flustered, he held out his hand to offer her the empty spot. *Why does she keep talking to me? I thought I'd been a complete asshole.* But then he remembered who her boyfriend was and figured she had a high tolerance for assholes.

He felt bad. "Yeah, sure."

She settled in and rooted through her backpack for her math textbook. Once it was on the table between them, she flipped through it until she came to her homework assignment. Her nimble fingers glided down the page.

When she caught him staring, they both looked away, embarrassed.

"I'm sorry," she said softly. "I just... Did you find anything else about my mom?"

He froze. Blood rushed to his face. "Umm..."

"I'm only asking because she died just after I was born, so I don't really know too much about her and I thought it was kind of neat that you found that article..."

"Uh, sure. Maybe. Here." He turned the paper around and pointed to the picture he had just found. "I was looking at this. Is that your mom?"

Becca's mouth gaped and both her hands flew to her heart. "Oh my god. Wow. What's she doing here?" Puzzled, she flipped to the front page. "In 1966?"

"I don't know," said James, coming around to her side of the table. "I just found it."

Standing side by side, they read the article together. It was an announcement about the 1966 Harvest Queen nominations. Bethany St. James, much like her daughter, had been a nominee.

"Your mom never mentioned she was running for queen?" he asked, pushing his glasses up the bridge of his nose.

She shook her head, face turning pale.

"Why not?" he asked. "Seems like a pretty big deal around here."

"We've never had a Harvest Festival. At least not while I've been around. This is before I was born."

"Couldn't have been that memorable then," James

said. "Funny, I thought I saw another article about a festival back in spring 1967. Couldn't have been very good if they had it in the *spring*."

Becca covered her mouth. He watched her aghast expression. It was starting to freak him out. "What's the matter?"

"My mom—" She paused to take a gulp of air. "She couldn't have done this kind of thing. She was really sick before I was born. I don't understand…"

Before James could ask her to explain, Travis Valcourt sauntered into the library. He had a single book tucked under his arm and gave a flirty wave to the old librarian, Mrs. Marley. Then he joined their table. James left the newspaper in Becca's hands and returned to his seat with his head down. He didn't want to converse with the lunk-head, so he buried himself in another book. But he was eager to ask Becca more about this.

Travis slipped an arm around her waist. She yelped in surprise and smacked him off, startling both young men.

Once she realized it was just Travis, she relaxed. "I'm sorry. It's just—" She tried to point to the paper, but Travis stuck a daisy in her face.

"A flower for you," he cooed in a baby voice.

"Travis," she said, with a warning tone.

"I didn't mean to end things like that the other night."

End things? James was starting to wonder if he should have gone to that stupid party. Becca might have needed a shoulder to cry on. *No,* he reminded himself. *No parties. In and out. No getting attached to any of these rednecks.*

"Look at this," Becca said, showing him the paper.

Travis leaned in, squinting. "'Bethany St. James,'" he read. "Hey, that's your mom."

"Yeah, I know."

"Cool."

"I didn't know she was nominated for Harvest Queen. Isn't that weird?"

He shrugged. "So? It was a long time ago."

"Did your dad mention anything about it?"

Travis scoffed. "My dad only cares about *present* business."

"But don't you think it's *weird?*" she pressed.

I do, thought James, unable to focus on his book. *I'll talk about it with you.* But he held his tongue, not wanting to attract Travis's attention.

Travis folded up the paper and pushed it onto James's side of the table. "I came here to talk about *us,*" he said.

"I don't think I want to talk about that right now," she said, crossing her arms.

"See? It's this kind of attitude that tells me you're not ready."

Not ready for what? James sat back, trying to think of an exit strategy, and then Travis gave him one.

"Hey, new guy? I need to talk to Becca *alone.* Mind, uh…?" Travis jerked a thumb toward the door.

"No, don't," said Becca, but James was already stuffing his notes and book into his bag.

"It's alright," he muttered, feeling flustered. "I should get ready for my next class."

"But—?"

James gave her a tight-lipped smile and hurried out.

* * *

James shouldn't have left, Becca thought. *I interrupted him and then Travis had to show up.* She pouted as her soon-to-be-ex boyfriend pulled up a seat. He rested an arm on the back of her chair, his fingers tracing her bra strap through her shirt.

"You know I care about you," he said, "but you're acting a little nuts."

"Excuse me?"

"Hey, I get it," he said. "You're gunning for the whole queen thing. It's a big deal, but only if you make it out to be."

"It's not that. It's—" She pointed to where the paper had been. Now it was gone and she felt her stomach drop. Did James run off with it? She needed to talk to him. He found something unusual, for sure. And she had to get home, because there was something she needed to check. She was going to have to do something she had never done before: Skip class.

She stared blankly at the table as all these thoughts raced through her brain, each one seeking a solution.

Travis sighed, shaking his head. "Is this about your mom? Did the new guy say something about her? Because I'll kick his ass."

She held up her hands. "No. Don't kick anyone's ass,"

she said a bit too loud. The librarian cleared her throat. Becca quieted down, lowering her head. "James is fine. He just showed me that article about my mom, but something's not right."

"That kinda news sounds fake," he said, running a hand through her hair. "It could be one of those joke newspapers the magic store used to sell. He's probably screwing with you."

"Why would he do that?"

He shrugged. "I don't know. He thinks he's a joker, remember. Or maybe he's trying to make a name for himself. Or…"

"Or what?"

Letting out a big, dramatic sigh, Travis rolled his eyes. "Or, I don't know… He's got a crush on you."

Becca blushed. "I doubt that. Pretty sure he hates everyone." She bit her lip. She couldn't wait until the final bell. She had to go home now, before afternoon classes started, or else she would be stuck at school for another couple of hours.

She jumped up and shoved all her books back into her bag. "I have to go."

"Go where?"

"Home."

"Why?"

She touched her stomach and tried to make a sick face. "Not feeling well."

"Huh," he said, pushing his chair back. "That's not like you. Wanna see the nurse?"

"No," she said.

"Or I could drive you home?"

"No," she repeated. He looked hurt by her emphasis. So she gave him a faint smile and touched his arm. "I'll be fine. Maybe the fresh air will help?"

"Okay, if you say so," he said. He pointed at her as she scurried out of the library just as James had. "But I'm calling later to check up on you!"

The librarian cleared her throat even louder this time.

Travis shrugged again. "What?"

* * *

Becca raced through the back door, dropping her backpack in the kitchen. She had run all the way home and bolted upstairs without thinking about what Gran would say when she got caught leaving school early.

Heart thundering against her ribcage and in her ears, she went into Gran's craft room, and though she was in a panic, she carefully moved the old woman's stitching projects from their "in-progress" spot atop an oak hope chest.

Inside the chest were all the things Gran had kept from Becca's mom. Her graduation cap and yearbook. A copy of her favorite romance novel, the corners worn off and the spine cracked from repeated readings. A couple of photos of people Becca didn't recognize. And tucked in a plastic sleeve along with a birth certificate was Bethany St. James's death certificate.

Hands shaking, Becca slid it from the sleeve and unfolded it atop a small sofa Gran stored in the room. She stared at the date. April 15, 1967 — one day after Becca was born.

As if mom was holding on so she could have me.

But now something nagged her. How would her mother — single, barely out of high school, and pregnant in a small town — get nominated for Harvest Queen? Going by James's newspaper article, she would have gotten pregnant just before the festival was supposed to have taken place. *But they moved it to spring? And then she died?*

She needed to ask James if he knew anything else.

And then she heard someone weeping in the next room.

Chapter 5

Becca crept out of the craft room and peered down the hall. Her bedroom door was wide open, sun pouring into the hallway. Dust motes twinkled in the beam of light. Opposite was her grandmother's room. The door was shut to only a crack, and as Becca neared the room, she could see the old woman lying on the bed.

Her back to the door, Gran was curled up on her side, legs tucked behind her. She wasn't sleeping; she never dozed off without one of her knit blankets, and here she was on top of the bedspread. She gripped her elbow with one hand and held a tissue to her face with the other.

Becca eased the door open for a better look. *Is Gran hurt?* She didn't want to startle her grandmother, but it was also unnerving to see the old woman like this. She never cried, even when she stepped on the loose nail on the deck and Becca had to call Sadie to pick them up and take them to the hospital for a tetanus shot.

But Becca also realized she was never home at this time on a weekday, and she suddenly felt like an intruder in her own home. Maybe this was the time of day her grandmother reserved for having a good cry.

Becca felt her face heat up and her armpits prickle. She wasn't supposed to be here. Gran was going to be upset that she had skipped school. And for what? A *death certificate?* What was the rush? It wasn't like her mom was going to get any *deader.*

She was about to scurry back to the craft room to put everything back and forget about whatever weird theory had started to form in her brain, when the floor underneath her foot creaked.

Gran lifted her head off the pillow. "Is someone there? Bethany?" She squinted at her watch. "What time is it?"

"Umm…" Becca hesitated.

With a grunt, Gran rolled over. She blinked her red-rimmed eyes a few times as if she couldn't properly focus. "You're back."

Becca opened her mouth. "I-I'm sorry—"

"I told you." The old woman sat up. "What did I say?"

Becca didn't know what she meant.

Gran smacked the back of her right hand into her left palm. "*I told you none of that queen bullshit!*"

"Gran?" Becca had never heard her grandmother swear before, aside from mutterings under her breath as she tackled some hardy weeds in the garden.

"Promise me you'll drop out. *Promise me.*"

Becca stood frozen, one hand holding the door frame. "Uhh…"

Her grandmother got off the bed and shuffled toward her. Her flowery shirt was tucked into the elastic waistband of her pants, and she had dirt sprinkled over her clothes like fairy dust. When she came to Becca and started smoothing down the girl's hair, she began to cry again.

"Oh!" she gasped. "Becca! I thought… I thought I saw something…"

Becca swallowed a hard, thick lump. "Mom?"

The tears stopped and Gran perked up. "I feel up for some lemonade!" Then she walked out of the room.

Becca paused in the doorway, looking around. Something fluttered on the bed where Gran had been laying. A newspaper. Checking over her shoulder, Becca picked it up. It was today's paper. On the front page was an announcement about the Harvest Festival — and a list of all the girls nominated for queen. Becca felt dizzy as her own photo stared back at her.

She looked a hell of a lot like her mother.

Maybe that's what scrambled up Gran's brain just now… Maybe that's what scrambled up my *brain.*

She bit her lip and tried to think.

"Beth…"

Becca put the paper down and found her grandmother in the bathroom. She was looking at herself in the mirror, making that same confused face again. Before Becca could gently correct her grandmother, Gran stared back at her reflection.

"Promise me — no more of this queen business." Her eyes watered up and her mouth trembled. "I don't want you to die."

Becca threw her arms around Gran and squeezed her. The old woman wept and shivered. Becca rubbed her back, trying to figure out just what the hell she was talking about.

"Gran... What do you mean 'die'?"

Gran took a deep breath and straightened up. She wiped her tears with the knuckle of her middle finger. "I'm making lemonade! Want some?"

* * *

Becca tried to enjoy her lemonade, but Gran added too much lemon flavor and it made Becca's lips pucker, and she desperately wanted to ask Gran about the last Harvest Festival and why there hadn't been another one in seventeen years.

She couldn't bear the thought of dragging Gran into her paranoid, not-even-a-theory theory that something strange might have happened to her mom. Something about the festival had upset her grandmother and Becca wasn't going to make it worse by asking unusual questions. At least not yet, not if she could help it.

So she told Gran that she was suffering from some severe menstrual cramps, but that she had taken an aspirin and just wanted to lay down in her room. She kept the death certificate with her and, curled up in bed, stared at it until Gran called her back down for supper.

After eating, she helped Gran with the dishes and they watched the news together. Soon enough, Gran stifled a yawn and put her knitting away.

"That's it for me," she said, heading upstairs. "Don't stay up too late, dear."

"I won't, Gran. Love you."

Once the old woman was washed-up and tucked away in bed, Becca went to the kitchen. She grabbed the phone book from under the counter and flipped through the M section until she found "Martin." Several Martins, to be exact. She poured herself another glass of lemonade and dialed each one until—

"Hello?" answered an older woman.

Becca glanced at the ticking black cat clock on the wall. It was after nine. "Hi, I'm sorry to call so late. Is James there?"

"Yes. May I ask who's calling?"

"Um, it's Becca. From school."

"Hello, Becca. I'll see if James is available. One second." The phone bumped something as James's mom set it down. "James! Someone from school is on the line… It's a girl… She said her name is Becca?"

Becca hated when parents answered, but she didn't want to be rude and hang up on Mrs. Martin.

James answered, sounding out of breath or annoyed — Becca couldn't tell the difference. "Hey," he said.

Speechless, she smacked her head. She spent all afternoon and night thinking about her mom and the festival and staring at that stupid death certificate, and now when she needed to express her concern to the only person who might possibly understand, she blanked. "Umm…"

"I'm in the middle of homework, so…"

"I think something bad happened to my mom." The words tumbled out in a mad rush.

"I thought you said your mom was sick?"

She nodded but stopped because he couldn't see her. "She died of leukemia in 1967."

"I'm sorry," he said.

She nodded again, trying to push away her tears. "She couldn't have been Harvest Queen. It couldn't have happened."

"I see," he said carefully.

Something in his tone said he knew something. "What do you know?"

"I'm not sure. I should go back over my notes."

"Okay." She fidgeted with the cord. "When?"

"How about after school at the public library?"

"Yeah," she said. "I'll be there."

* * *

James laid awake until the early morning hours. He stared at the popcorn ceiling and studied every nook and cranny of the light fixture above. The previous family had installed a Raggedy Ann light, and as weird as it was to be a seventeen-year-old guy sleeping in what was once a little girl's bedroom, neither James nor his mom could figure out how to install a new light. He would have been okay with a bare lightbulb, just to save his mother from spending her hard-earned dollars to spruce up his room.

Because this — *this rented house, this high school, this stupid town* — was temporary to James.

He rolled over to see the calendar pinned to his wall. It was already flipped to December '84. He had circled the last day of school. That was his deadline to get out of this place. If his mother hadn't caught him off guard at the end of the last semester, he would have put his plan into gear then, so as not to have to start at Morganville High at all.

Nothing against the school, but to James, it was filled with troglodyte country boys who pasted Confederate flag stickers on their bumpers and revved their truck engines at him when he crossed the street. They didn't even know him, but on the other hand, James didn't want to know any of them.

He just wanted to move back to the city.

And then Becca St. James called him, and though she wanted to talk about her mom, he had never felt so excited about something that had to do with this lame town.

There was a dark undertone to their meeting, however. Becca's mother, Bethany, had died during the year of the last Harvest Festival, and from what he gathered from his research, she wasn't the first Harvest Queen to die young.

Chapter 6

Wednesday night, Becca ate a quick dinner with her Gran and then filled her backpack with notebooks and pens. She had to at least give the illusion that she was studying. But before she could head out the door, Travis called.

"Hey," he drawled.

Normally, his deep voice purring in her ear would be enough to set her heart on fire, but tonight he was keeping her from getting to the library.

"Hi," she said.

"Didn't see you at school yesterday."

"I was there." *You just didn't look for me.*

Travis had an amazing ability to get out of trouble by avoiding it. His friends joked that he got it from his dad. Nothing bad ever stuck to the Valcourt men.

She heard him scratch the back of his head while he hung on the line. For a moment, she worried he was going to ask what she was up to, and she didn't want to tell him about her library plans with James, nor did she want to lie to her boyfriend about meeting another guy. Even though there was nothing going on between her and the new guy, lying about it seemed like cheating.

"I just wanted to say sorry," he said. "You know, for the whole not thinking you're ready thing."

"It's fine," she said.

He lowered his voice. "Is your grandma on the line?"

"We don't have another line," she said.

"Oh, right." Travis often forgot his family was one of the few in town that had nice extras, like more than one phone line, air conditioning, and a three-car garage. "Okay, well, look — I know you wanna do it, but I want it to be special for you."

She repressed a sigh. "Was your first time special?"

"It was alright, I guess. But I want your first time to be better than that, okay?"

A blush crept up her chest and warmed her face. "Okay."

"So … you're not mad at me?" She could hear his smile.

"No, I guess not," she said.

He let out a deep breath that crackled through the receiver. "So you'll sit with us at lunch tomorrow?"

"Yeah."

"Good… I missed you."

"I missed you too," she said, smiling back. She was about to hang up when Travis asked one more thing.

"Hey, how about I pick you up and we go grab a burger?"

"Oh." *Damn it.* "I just ate."

"That's okay. I'll buy ya a milkshake."

"I shouldn't. I have a lot of studying to do." The lies were starting. How easily that one slipped out. Cringing, she grabbed her head.

"I'll bring one over," he said. "Just give me 15 minutes and I'll be right there. Maybe you could help me with this week's bio homework."

She stared at the clock on the wall. If she didn't get moving, she was going to be late to meet up with James. *Would he wait for me? For how long?* "I really can't."

"Why not?" He sounded hurt.

"Gran's in bed. I don't want to wake her."

"We can sit on your porch. I'll be quiet."

"I don't think so…"

"Come on, babe," he whispered.

She bit her lip, warmth spreading between her legs and shame everywhere else.

"Is that a yes?"

"I really can't. But I'll see you tomorrow, okay? Bye."

She hung up the phone before she could change her mind. Leaning against the wall, she considered calling him back. It would be so much easier.

No, she told herself. *I need to know what happened to my mom.*

* * *

On the walk to the library, the sun set and the sky went from hazy pink to purple to black. Streetlights flickered on slowly as Becca stepped on fallen leaves, enjoying the crunch they made. She tried not to think about Travis and wondered about James instead.

What did he like to do for fun? Did he have a girlfriend in the city? Could someone so nerdy be a good kisser?

Her face burned. If James asked why she was so red, she would say it was from the walk. Not from thinking about things that were none of her business.

She crossed the street from the elementary school and past the former kindergarten. There was no need to have a separate facility for the little kids anymore. The population had taken such a nosedive in the last few years that there were very few young families left, and the ones that remained could squeeze their children into a single class.

She hurried past the old convent, another building no longer used for its original purpose. It housed nuns up until the 1950s, but since then, it had been turned into a condo. Something about a bunch of nuns clustered in the dark and foreboding units behind the Catholic church spooked her. Maybe because the reflections on the windows always looked like moving faces.

It made her think of the faded paint on the grain elevator. From a distance, it almost looked like the building had eyes.

She tightened her grip on her backpack and cut

through the church grounds. Footpaths curved around big, deciduous trees and small flower beds. All the flowers had died off, waiting for the first dump of snow that usually came at the end of October. Once she made it through the park, she just had to cross main street and she would be at the library.

Up ahead, one of the benches was occupied. She might have passed right by without a second thought — until she saw who was there. The homeless guy was out tonight. One leg bent at the knee crossed over the other. His arms were spread across the back of the bench, one hand held a bottle hidden in a paper bag.

Becca watched him from the corner of her eye. He was definitely staring at her, his head turning as she passed by. He was known to yell horrible things at women, or openly spit and scratch his balls. At the moment, he took turns smoking and sipping from his bottle. His lips were curled around his cigarette, ready to mouth off, but with her head down, Becca passed him unscathed.

Or so she thought.

"What?!" he barked. Becca jumped. "Pretending you don't see me? *You see me!"*

Becca cowered, keeping her head down. She was almost out of the park and on the main sidewalk. *Almost there.*

The homeless guy leapt off the bench. He hurled his bottle down. The glass shattered. Becca yelped and spun around. He pointed his finger.

"You see me," he slurred. "Think yer better than me?"

She shyly shook her head and turned to go. Main street suddenly felt a million miles away. She couldn't see through the trees or around the statue of Christ that welcomed people in. Darkness closed around her, and the one streetlight above wasn't enough to scare the bad guys away, or even just this one guy.

"Come here a second," he said, lowering his voice.

Becca kept walking.

"I got somethin' to show you."

She didn't care what it was, though she feared it would be small and pink and sticking out of his fly. And if that was the case, she was certain she did not want to see it.

"I said come here!"

Feet thumping on the pavement, he ran up behind her and grabbed her arm. His unshaven face and nose were dimpled with a severe case of rosacea, cheeks bloated from years of alcohol abuse.

"Get offa me!" she screamed.

He clutched her bag. His newspaper smacked her in the face. "Just hold it, will ya?"

She shrieked. "No! Lemme go! Stop!"

She twisted around, trying to get away. Arms snaked around her waist, he dragged her back toward the bench. His breath was foul, his fingers greasy on her arms. He grunted as she fought back.

"I just gotta—"

"Hey! Leave her alone!"

Becca looked up. It was James, sloughing off his backpack before charging at them. With a squeak, Becca pulled away. James shoved the man, sending him tumbling onto the bench as Becca fell to the ground.

"Fucking kids," the man croaked.

"Get out of here!" James yelled. "Or I'll— I'll beat your ass!"

The man wiped his ruddy nose on the back of his hand. He studied James and looked back at Becca. For a moment, she was certain he was going to attack, but he began to laugh and shake his head.

"Fuckin' kids," he muttered again. He picked up his paper and limped away.

Becca pushed herself up. Her hip ached from hitting the pavement. She grimaced, feeling unbalanced, and then overcorrected, stumbling. James caught her. She stared into his dark blue eyes hidden behind his glasses and shaggy hair. He blinked nervously and let her go.

"Sorry!" they blurted at the same time.

Collecting their bags, Becca and James hurried out of the park. They kept looking back to make sure they weren't being followed. Neither one spoke until they made it to the library.

Once they were within the library's warm, inviting glow, Becca leaned against the storefront-style window and let out a shaky breath.

"Are you okay?" James asked.

She nodded, but she sure didn't feel okay.

"Maybe we should call the police?"

"I'll live."

"Yeah, but he grabbed you. He was trying to take you

somewhere. That's assault, that's kidnapping."

"But he didn't. I'm fine. I don't want to relive it, okay? Let's just get on with this."

"As long as you're sure."

"I'm sure."

"I still think—"

She grabbed his arm, squeezing it to make him look at her and not the phone booth nearby. "Please, James?"

"Okay," he said, giving her a shaky smile. "Glad he didn't challenge me." He held up his fists, thumbs tucked in. "I've never hit anyone in my life."

"I think you would've broken your thumbs," she said, returning his smile.

"Let's not do that again," he said. "What did he want anyway?" James held the door open for her and they went inside.

Mr. Handy the librarian, in his maroon sweater vest and neatly trimmed mustache, gave them both a wave and welcomed them in. Already Becca felt safer, even though she and James were the only patrons there.

"I don't know," said Becca as they found a table in the back. "Maybe my backpack?" She opened it up and took out a notebook.

James peeked inside. "Because of all your fine Fabergé notebooks?" he teased.

She elbowed him. "Real funny. Can we just forget about it for now? I kinda want to talk about…" *My mom.*

"Yeah, of course." He cleared his throat. "Not sure how helpful any of this will be, but there were a couple of odd things."

She uncapped her pen, ready to take notes. "Like what?"

"This year's festival isn't a one-off and neither was the one in 1967, but it was supposed to happen a few months earlier. Town council postponed it for some reason. I can't figure out why they would move a *Harvest* Festival to the spring, though. Doesn't make sense."

She scribbled down the years. "How many other festivals have there been?"

"Uh…" He opened his own notebook and flipped through. "There was one in 1949 and another in 1933. The earliest I could find goes back to 1916."

Becca again wrote down the years. "And they were all called the Harvest Festival?"

"Yeah."

"And did they all have a queen?"

He peered at her over his glasses. "Yeah, and you're not going to like this." He pushed his notebook to her.

Hand shaking, Becca turned it around and scanned it.

> *1916 – Farm wife Millie Sawyer – MISSING*
> *1933 – Teacher Marsha McCreedy – MURDERED*
> *1949 – New bride Viola Pettit – MURDERED*
> *1967 – High school grad Beth St. James …*

Becca fixated on her mother's name. "You didn't write anything in about…"

"I didn't know what to write," he said, taking his notes back.

"What do you mean?"

He shrugged. "I don't know. I just thought… Have you seen her, uh, death certificate?"

"I have it." She dug it out and handed it to him; he rubbed his chin as he looked it over.

"It doesn't say."

"It doesn't say what?"

"Her cause of death."

Scowling, she snatched it back. "You don't need a certificate to tell you that. She had leukemia. She was sick while she was pregnant with me and died after giving birth. She was too weak to hold on any longer after that."

"I don't think that's true," he said. "And I'm pretty sure if you really believed that, you wouldn't be here right now."

"What then?"

He handed her a folder from his bag. She opened it. Inside were photocopied clippings of news articles about the 1966 festival and the coronation event.

Bethany St. James was in dozens of photos. She beamed and waved like a queen in the earlier ones, but as they neared the date of the festival, she smiled less and less. One thing Becca noticed was that she didn't look sick at all.

She looked pissed off.

James pointed to the list of queens. "I think she found out what happened to the others."

Chapter 7

After going over James's notes and taking down her own, Becca stared at the table. James let her think in silence, but when Mr. Handy came around to give them a fifteen-minute warning, Becca snapped out of it. *How had they spent three hours going over this?*

James called his mom while Becca waited at the door. She hugged her backpack while trying to process everything she had learned. Her ghostly reflection stared back at her, making it difficult to watch for the homeless guy.

Every single Harvest Queen had died after her coronation. Becca had tried to argue that the one who went missing in 1916 might have just moved away, but James insisted it was too much of a coincidence. A mysterious disappearance was suspicious. There was something insidious about the festival.

The door squealed open as James joined her in the vestibule. "Mr. Handy said we could wait here until my mom comes." He noticed her shivering. "Cold?"

He had already slipped his jacket off and handed it to her before she could refuse. "No, that's—" She smiled as he placed the warm fabric over her shoulders. "Thanks," she said. "So what do you think happened to them?"

"You mean, how could those people die right after being queen?"

"Yeah, what are the chances?"

"All I know is that I wouldn't want to be Harvest Queen."

The tension building up inside Becca boiled over and she burst into tears, covering her quivering lip. She didn't want to be queen either, but the scholarship...

"Oh, jeez," he muttered. "I forgot."

Tremors wracked her body. She dropped her backpack and sat down.

James looked around awkwardly before kneeling beside her. In the narrow space, she smelled the fresh soap on his skin. "You're probably right. It's just a weird coincidence. You said it yourself — your mom was sick. Nothing shady happened there."

Tears streamed down her rosy cheeks. "I don't know if that's true anymore."

He touched her shoulder. "What're you saying?"

"Something my Gran said..." *I don't want you to die.* "She knows something."

"Can you ask her?"

Becca wiped her eyes. "I don't know. She's … not all there some of the time."

"That could work for us."

"She thought I was my mom the other day."

"Even better."

"No," she said. "I don't like that look in your eye."

"What look?"

"Like you want to interrogate a harmless, old woman."

"I wouldn't do that," he said. "I meant we could ask her together."

"I don't think that's a good idea." She grabbed her things and stood up at the same time he did. Her body bumped against him as she let herself out. "Bye."

"Hey." He went after her. "Wait!"

She stopped at the crosswalk. The thought of cutting through the park made the hairs on the back of her neck rise. The homeless man could still be out there.

James stood beside her. His shirt was rumpled, and his sleeves were rolled up to his elbows. He looked like a frazzled young professor. "I'm sorry. I didn't mean to … act like a jerk," he said.

"I don't think you're a j—"

"I'm an asshole."

"No, you're n—"

He held out his arms, presenting himself to main street. "I'm a prick. I'm a piece of shit. I'm a dick. I'm a—"

She ran up and covered his mouth. "Stop! Don't say that. You're not any of those things."

"But I am still unlikeable, right? I don't want to ruin

my reputation."

"Shut up," she said, unable to keep from smiling. *"I like you. It's your 'grandmother interrogation' idea I don't care for."*

"That's fair," he said.

"And we don't even know what we're doing or what any of this means."

"Should we go to the police?"

"It's probably nothing."

"You're right," he said. "I'll just stick to writing my stupid report."

"It's not like we're going to uncover Watergate," she teased.

They exchanged a smile and nervously looked down at the sidewalk. After an awkward pause, he said, "Let me take you home."

She stared across the street at the church park. The homeless guy had abandoned the bench, but beyond it, thick trees hid all shapes and shadows. Becca felt like she was being watched.

"Okay."

* * *

Mrs. Martin parked her wood-paneled station wagon in front of Gran's bungalow and wished Becca a goodnight. Then she nudged James to get out of the car and walk Becca to the door.

"That's okay," said Becca. "I can manage."

Caught between a rock and his mother, James climbed out of the car and walked Becca to her house.

"Don't mind my mom," he said. "She's a little—"

Becca touched his arm to stop him. "She seems nice."

"Thanks." He turned to leave, but Becca held onto his arm. His face started to burn as he felt his mom staring at them, analyzing their every move.

"I don't think I can talk to my grandmother about any of this," she said. "She's not well…"

He nodded, listening.

"But that doesn't mean I want to stop digging."

"Me neither. So what then?"

She chewed on her lip. "I think I might know someone else we can talk to — Gran's friend, Sadie."

He clapped his hands together. "Let's do it."

"But let me ask first, okay?"

"Sure." He said goodbye and turned to walk away.

"Wait," she said. "Don't you want your jacket back?"

"Oh, yeah, of course," he said sheepishly.

She took it off and handed it back.

As their hands collided in the exchange, he brushed a finger over her knuckles and leaned in close enough to whisper, "I think you'd make a great queen, but something tells me it might be hazardous to your health."

"Way ahead of you," she said. "First thing tomorrow, I'm dropping out."

* * *

"What do you mean you won't let me quit?"

Becca stood in the middle of the school parking lot and slammed Travis's car door shut. He reached into the backseat for his English textbook, a dog-eared copy of *Romeo & Juliet*, when she started to panic.

Travis had picked her up that morning to take her to school. He brought Gran some fresh-baked muffins from the grocery store and made polite conversation with her while Becca finished her breakfast. Gran beamed at his attention, and Becca couldn't help smiling. He was so kind to her grandmother and seemed really engaged in their conversation about gardening (Gran's favorite topic). He could be so damn charming sometimes.

After Gran said goodbye and went out to work on her rose bushes, Becca pulled Travis into the living room where Gran couldn't see them, and kissed him. He slid his hands around her waist and grinned. "Guess you're not mad at me anymore, huh?"

She rolled her eyes. "I wasn't mad, just … distracted."

"I bet," he said. "This Harvest Queen thing has really got you stressed out. But don't worry, I know how to relieve stress." He popped open the button on her jeans and eased the zipper down.

The mere mention of the Harvest Queen role filled her stomach with ice water. "No…"

"I know you want it."

"Travis!" She pried his hands away. *"Gran is outside."*

"So?" he said. "How loud do you think you're gonna be?" He winked.

She backed up against Gran's cabinet of knick-knacks. The little ceramic figurines inside rattled, warning her that something was about to get broken. *"We can't."*

"Says who?" He pressed her against the shelf, sliding his hands down her backside and cupping her ass cheeks. His mouth nuzzled against her neck. "Come on, baby… You need this. *We* need this."

Moaning, she pulled away. *"Time for school,"* she said.

With a dramatic sigh, he cocked his head back. "Whatever."

So they were already off to a rocky start when Becca brought up the Harvest Festival on the drive to school. Her fingernails traced the edges of her notebook, which contained the notes she copied from James. She reviewed them after coming home last night and had decided the scholarship wasn't worth risking her life, even if it was all a coincidence.

Travis squeezed her leg as he drove with one hand on the steering wheel. The awkward silence between them was thick by the time he parked in his usual spot at school. That's when Becca piped up.

"Um, I've been thinking… I'm going to take my name out of the competition."

"What competition? You write another essay for fun?"

"No — for Harvest Queen. I don't think I'm right for it."

He rolled his head around to face her. "You're just getting cold feet. You're totally right for it. My dad even says so."

"I just don't think it's a good use of my time," she said, gripping the notebook. "Do you think you could talk to your dad for me? Tell him I'm sorry and that—?"

Travis cut her off. "Well, you can tell him yourself at dinner Friday night."

"Dinner?"

"Yeah, mom wanted me to invite you over. They haven't seen you since August long. They're starting to think I don't have a girlfriend anymore."

"I'm still your—"

He cut her off again. "Well, you haven't been acting like it. Hanging around with the new guy..." he mumbled. She was about to deny it when he stopped her. "Don't even. Heath saw you guys at the library last night."

Becca's jaw dropped. She knew for a fact that she and James were the only people there last night, and she had never seen Heath step inside a library. "Your friends are spying on me?"

"They're not spying, Becca," he said. "Heath and Candace were out for a walk, and they saw you and the new kid go in together."

"We were studying," she said. "Where else would we go?" Even though his accusing tone was off the charts, she thought about making him jealous — *Where do you expect us to go? His bedroom?*

He ran a hand through his slick hair. "I'm not mad. If you want someone to study with, you can call me."

And lower my average by two whole letter grades?

She felt guilty for thinking that way. She looked down at her lap.

"You could've at least told me."

"Told you what? I said I was studying."

"Yeah, but you didn't say with *who*. And you know I don't like that guy."

"I didn't know that," she lied. "What's wrong with him?"

He frowned. "You get this weird look in your eye."

"What look?"

"Like you're soft on him or something."

"He's new. He doesn't have any friends. I'm just trying to help."

"I think you've helped enough," he grumbled.

"What does that mean?"

"It means you'd better stop spending time with him."

She was shocked that in mere minutes he could change from Gran's biggest fan to such a jealous boyfriend stereotype. "You're jealous."

He twisted around in the bucket seat to stare at her. "You're damn right I am. You're spending all your time with this guy."

"It was one night," she said, grabbing her head. *Am I going crazy?* "You don't even like the library!"

He grabbed her hands. "But I like *you*. Doesn't that count for something? And I thought we wanted to be together. I thought you wanted to lose your virginity to me?" He paused, letting her stew on that. "I want to be your boyfriend, Becca, I really do, but you gotta stop hanging out with other guys, or—"

"Or what?" she challenged.

He sighed again, looking out the window. "Or I'm gonna think you don't want to be with me anymore."

"That's not true—"

The bell rang. Students jumped out of their cars, stubbing out cigarettes and chowing down their breakfast sandwiches on their way to class. Becca wasn't done with this conversation, but she couldn't miss another class this week, and because Mr. Walsh was teaching math this morning, she was already late.

"Travis, I'm sorry," she said. "I didn't mean to hurt you."

He shrugged, pouting.

"I don't need to see James anymore, okay? He's just been doing some research into the festival and—"

"I don't care what he's doing as long as it doesn't have anything to do with you," he said sharply.

She continued, rambling on as she opened the door. "—and the whole Harvest Queen scholarship has been distracting me from our time together, and that's why I think I'd better quit."

"I won't let you quit," he said.

"What do you mean you won't let me quit?"

They slammed their doors. Wincing, Travis scratched the back of his neck with his book. "Quitters never win, Becca. I know you can win this."

"I don't want to win," she said. "I don't care."

"Well, I care *for you* then. You gotta stick with it, even

if it seems hard. Besides…" He put an arm around her neck and shoulders as they converged toward the school. The final bell buzzed, and Mr. Mac stood on the steps, pointing to his watch. "…my dad says you're a shoo-in."

Chapter 8

Becca curled the phone line around her finger, keeping an eye out for Gran, who was prone to waking up in the night and wandering down to the kitchen for a glass of milk.

It was after eleven, and Becca knew she should have been in bed. If not sleeping, then reading a book. But Travis's words bothered her all day and into the night, and as she laid down and closed her eyes, she couldn't shut her brain off. She had to talk to someone, and the only person that seemed right was James.

It also felt wrong, but in a way she found strangely exciting.

"... and then Travis said his dad said I'm a shoo-in," she finished. "I don't want to be a shoo-in. I want to forget about this."

"We can't forget," James said. "Even if you find a way to quit, someone else will be queen and she'll end up dead."

"We don't know that…"

"Look at the history, the facts… Something messed up has been happening in this town and—" He stopped abruptly. Papers rustled on his end. "Yes! This! Okay, I did a deep dive into the town's financials…"

That sounded horribly boring and dry even to Becca.

"…and it looks like they announce one of these festivals when the town's economy is tanking."

"It's supposed to be a morale booster," she said.

"Maybe, sure, but it must be one hell of an economic booster too, because for years afterward, the town sees a huge uptick in new business and increased cash flow. Even the population gets a bump."

Becca pinched the bridge of her nose. "Let me see if I understand: A girl dies and the town gets rich?"

"Exactly."

"Almost like a human sacrifice."

"Yes."

Becca had to lean against the wall for support. This was so ridiculous and terrifying at the same time. "People don't do that anymore."

"It seems like Morganville might."

"I think you're reaching, James," she said coldly. Who the hell was he to accuse her hometown of sacrificing people? He was just the new guy. All he was doing was stirring up trouble, not uncovering a conspiracy.

"And I think you're scared, Becca," he challenged. "You don't want it to be true."

"Of course not! It's stupid! It's awful!" A floorboard squeaked above. Either the house was making a settling noise or Gran heard her ranting. Becca lowered her voice. "It's just not true."

"Then we have to keep digging until we know for sure."

I don't want to. Can't I just bury my head in the sand and wait for this to blow over?

But she couldn't do that because James was right. They had to be sure. *She* had to be sure. "I don't like this."

"I don't either," he said. "Is there any way you can beg Mr. Valcourt to let you off the hook?"

She began to unravel her hand from the cord. Red lines formed on her skin where she had wound it too tight. "Maybe. I'm having dinner at Travis's house on Friday. I'm going to ask him then."

"Don't just ask. Beg."

* * *

At the sound of the final bell on Friday, Becca ran out of class. She had worn her gym shoes for just the occasion and finished most of her homework in study hall and over her lunch period just so she wouldn't have to lug a heavy backpack with her.

As she stepped onto the front pavilion, she pulled her long brown hair into a ponytail and started jogging.

The Red Lion Retirement Village wasn't far from her house, but Becca had a busy Friday planned. She needed to speak to Gran's friend Sadie and still have enough time to get home, get dressed, and get to Travis's house for dinner — and not be late because his mom was a stickler for that kind of thing.

So she ran. The autumn sun warmed her face as she trampled through fallen leaves. Even with all the questions she planned to ask Sadie racing through her head, she felt better doing something active instead of staring at the same old newspaper clippings.

We don't sacrifice people here. That's not a thing.

I've lived here my entire life. Nothing like that has ever happened.

Those other queens only share that weird coincidence. Just a coincidence. My mom wasn't killed. She was sick.

By the time she crossed the street to the Red Lion, Becca had just about talked herself out of going in. James's theory was way too radical for her small, conservative town. He was spouting some Satanic panic–type bullshit. There was no way it was possible.

So just when she had decided she wasn't going to bother Sadie, James blew past her on his bike. He flashed her a smile as he skidded to a stop. He hid his bike behind a bush as Becca marched up to him.

"What are you doing here?" she demanded, though she already knew.

"I'm checking up on the last person standing with any connection to the 1966 town council," he said. "Well, aside from your grandmother."

She crossed her arms. He finally had his facts wrong.

"My grandmother was never on town council. She hates politics."

He reached into his bag and pulled out a ledger. He held it open at a page that included the headshots of the reeve and his six councilmen and women. Among them was Dorothy St. James, smiling up at the corner of the page.

Becca didn't take the ledger from him. Her hands were shaking too badly. She balled them into fists and turned her back on him, heading inside.

"Hey, hey, hey!" he called, following her in. "I know you're here to talk to Sadie Frances. I am too, so we'd better get our story straight."

"What story? I don't need a story to talk to my grandma's friend. She'll talk to *me*, not *you*."

He grinned. "Good, even better if we work together."

Becca sighed, rolling her head back. Before she could make a full rotation, she stopped herself — her reflection in the glass door reminded her of Travis's dismissive attitude and because she knew all too well how it made her feel when Travis did it to her, she didn't want to do it to James.

"It's not a good idea," she said. "Sadie's seventy-two. I don't want to stress her out."

"I get that, and I get that you don't want to stress out your grandma either," said James, "but at some point, these older people are going to have to account for the totally weird shit that went down under their watch and in their town."

"Fine. But *I* ask the questions. You're just ... along for the ride."

After passing the check-in desk, Becca and James went down one of the long hallways to Sadie's room. She wasn't there but had left her door open.

Spider plants hung in macrame in every corner. Photos of chubby-cheeked grandchildren were scattered around on her bureau and nightstand. A pink housecoat hung off a coat rack and the thermostat was set on high.

"Guess she's busy?" said James.

Becca pointed at the cross-stitched sign on her door.

IF I AIN'T DEAD, I'M DANCING.

"Let's go."

The basement had been converted into an activity center, even though the home was across the street from the town's community hall. The seniors had decided years ago that they weren't going to bust their asses crossing the boulevard in the icy wintertime, so if the nursing staff wanted them to exercise, they were going to have to come up with a plan closer to home.

The converted basement had room for dancing and karaoke, shuffleboard, and yoga. Lines had been painted around the perimeter to mark off an indoor track. A few of the seniors walked on it, even one old gentleman in a wheelchair and another pushing a walker.

Becca and James waited for one of the men to pass before crossing the track to where a group of septuagenarian ladies in spandex and headbands danced along to an aerobics video. In the middle of them, barking orders and encouragement was Sadie Frances.

Sadie was small and hunched over in her wheelchair, but she had the biggest smile and the sharpest blue eyes. Her hair was permed and tinted purple, and though she couldn't get up on her feet, she was dancing and swinging her arms harder than any of the others.

"Come on, girls! Show me what you got! I saw more action in WWII!"

The other women hooted and laughed.

Then Sadie wheeled around and pointed two fingers at Becca and James. "You're a little young for my class," she said.

Becca smiled. "We're not here to dance. I wanted to ask you some questions about—"

Sadie cut a finger across her throat. Her nails were long, pointed, and painted bright pink. "Nope. You're either in or you're out." Becca and James exchanged a nervous glance, and before they could discuss what they should do, Sadie barked at them and snapped her finger. "Get out then. This ain't a zoo!"

"What does that mean?" James muttered.

"It means we're not here to watch. Come on."

Becca pulled James into the mix of old ladies and after a few moments of watching them, she picked up on their routine. The other women applauded her for joining. Becca grinned, nudging James.

"It's not that hard," she said.

"I've got two left feet," he replied. "I'll just wait outside…"

She grabbed his hand before he could get away, interlocking her fingers with his. "Come on. Don't be a chicken."

He stammered but didn't try to pull away. As she dove back into the routine, she moved his arm up and down for him. With the other hanging limply at his side, she reached around and started moving that too.

Giving him a goofy grin, she started making him dance along with her. Finally, trying to repress a smile, he half-heartedly tried to keep up with Becca and the older women.

By their third and final routine, James was starting to get into it. Sweating, he whipped off his jacket and tossed it aside. For the first time, Becca could see his long, muscular arms and the way his t-shirt hung off his hunched shoulders.

At last, Sadie clapped her hands and declared the class over. She punched a button on the VCR and her tape popped out.

Panting, Becca and James smiled sheepishly at each other.

"That wasn't so bad," she said, punching his shoulder.

"It was … okay, I guess," he said.

Sadie rolled in between them. "I need a shower." An older gent jogging by whistled and Sadie barked, "Oh, to hell with ya, Bill!"

Becca checked her watch. The aerobics ate up twenty

precious minutes. She was going to be crunched for time getting to Travis's house. "We really need to talk to you now," she said.

The old woman beckoned them to follow.

Chapter 9

*S*adie rolled into the far corner of her room, where she selected a towel from her bureau drawer. She dabbed at her face and under her arms. "I think I know why you're here," she said.

"You do?"

Sadie winked. "Dottie told me. You're up for Harvest Queen. What a treat."

But Sadie didn't smile. The lines around her mouth and eyes crinkled into a grimace, and even her words sounded a little sarcastic.

"Your husband was on town council in 1966," said James.

"That's right," she said, before he could continue. She rolled over to her nightstand and picked up a framed picture of a balding man resting his head on his fist. "My sweet Gerry. Rest in peace."

"That was the last year there was a Harvest Festival," said Becca.

"That's right. And it was a good one too." She looked down at the photo.

Becca clenched her fists. *Look me in the eye and tell me something new.* "My mom—" she began, but James cut her off with a wave.

"Why doesn't the town have a festival every year?" he asked. "Seems like a good boost to the economy."

"Economy, schmonomy," she grumbled. "It's about people and togetherness and all that baloney."

"Why not have it every year then?"

"It's a lotta work. Practically killed my Gerry when they had to postpone the damn thing."

"What for?"

Sadie grunted and waved her hand about. "The queen got in the family way… Unmarried too."

"Family way?" questioned James. "You mean—?"

"She was going to have a baby," said Becca. "You postponed it for her?"

"*I* didn't, but the council did." She raised her chin up high. "It was *my* recommendation however."

"That was my mom."

"I remember," she said.

"She was pregnant with me."

"I figured as much."

Becca licked her lips and decided to try something. "And then she was murdered?"

Sadie didn't blink. "It was a real shame."

Becca went numb from the tips of her toes to her scalp. Mixed feelings washed over her until she thought she was going to drown in them.

My mom was murdered.

Because she was Harvest Queen.

Oh, no. Oh, shit. Oh—

James hooked his arm through hers, steadying her before she could sink down to the floor. He wrapped his hand around hers, stroking her knuckles in the soothing way he had the other night.

"What happened exactly?" he asked Sadie.

Sadie rubbed her chin. "Well, that was a long time ago. My memory doesn't play nice anymore. You should ask Dottie."

Becca took a gulp of stale air. The little room was too stuffy, and her shirt collar fit too snugly. "Gran's memory is pretty much gone these days, so that's why I was hoping you could answer my questions."

"I bet you have many," she said, reaching out and clasping Becca's free hand. "You're such a beautiful girl, just like your mother." She slyly glanced at James and smiled. "Is this cool cat your *new boyfriend?*"

"Uhh…" James tried to protest, but Sadie grabbed his hand too and gave him a wink.

"I don't know what happened to that Travis hunk, but take care of this girl, y'hear? The queen must be spoiled rotten before the big day."

"What happens on the big day?" he asked.

Sadie let go and wagged her finger. "Wouldn't you like to know."

James crouched down. "I would actually, ma'am."

"I won't spoil the surprise," she said. "Not this time."

"When did you spoil the surprise, Sadie?" Becca asked.

Sadie wheeled back to her husband's photo. "I let it slip to your mum and she went off and got pregnant. She should've known that wasn't going to stop things."

"Stop what?" Becca and James asked in unison.

"The Harvest Festival, dear." Sadie tilted her head and stared at them. Her bright blue eyes glazed over and her pink lipstick smile was almost cartoonish on her weathered face. "Being queen is a civic duty. The festival is going to happen whether you want it or not."

* * *

"We're going around in circles," muttered James after they left Sadie's room.

"And I have a million *more* questions," said Becca, hesitating. She clasped a hand to her forehead. "My mom—"

"I know," he said. "But that woman isn't going to give us any more info, and if we keep pushing, she might tell someone."

"We *should* tell someone! *My mother was murdered!*"

Shushing her, James led her down the hall and out of the Red Lion. She was shaking by the time they got outside. It was dusk and the air had cooled off. When the chill hit her, Becca felt her senses return.

"Sorry," she muttered.

"It's okay," he said. "She dropped a huge bomb on you. Maybe we should, uh, get some dinner and talk this over?"

Becca wanted nothing more than to grab a burger and dig into the facts with James, but she had plans.

She checked her watch. It was half-past five. *Where did the time go?* She promised Travis she would be there at six. She was going to have to run straight home. "Sorry, I have to run," she said. "I'm having dinner with Travis's parents, but I need to go home first."

"Wait," said James. "I can get you there on my bike." He dragged it out from behind the bushes and patted the handlebars. "Hop on."

"Is it safe?"

He squinted, his cheekbones pushing his frames up. "You're running around trying to solve a mystery and you're worried about bike safety?"

"No, it's not…" She was worried about being so close to James, because her attraction to him was growing with every minute they spent together. Riding in his lap all the way home would be one more thing that was going to make her confused about her feelings.

She looked over her shoulder, trying to figure out what to do, when the homeless guy ambled out from behind a thick tree. As soon as he spotted them, he stabbed a finger in the air.

"Hey, you!"

Becca didn't even think. She grabbed James's bike. James climbed on and started pedaling. She jumped on the handlebars and cried, *"Go!"*

As they raced away from the Red Lion, Becca twisted her head around to see the homeless guy. He was shouting at them but didn't give chase. Still, she didn't feel safe until they put enough distance between them that she couldn't see him anymore.

James slowed as she directed him to turn down her street.

"I was just thinking..." he began.

"About what?"

"How did you meet Travis?"

She laughed. "How does anyone here meet? We've been going to school together since we were five."

"That's a long time," he said. "You ever, uh, wish you could meet someone new?"

"Sure," she said. "I like Travis, but..."

"But?"

"But I'm planning to go to college in the city. Travis has already said he's not interested."

"Oh," he said.

"What I *really* want is to get into med school. But I don't know if that's ever going to happen."

"Why not?"

"Well... maybe if I wasn't running all over town with you I could be studying harder."

He stopped the bike in front of Gran's house. "Sorry."

That came out wrong. "No, I mean—"

"It's okay. Maybe we're making too much of this Harvest thing. I should've just kept it to myself."

A few streets over, a car engine roared.

"No." She jumped off the bike and grabbed his hands, still wrapped around the handlebars. "No, this is important. We have to keep going and... And I like spending time with you."

His face turned red. "Oh, yeah, same. I like—"

Bright headlights turned the corner and a black vehicle rumbled toward them. It came to a screech and the driver laid on the horn. Bad Company blasted through the open windows. Travis stuck his head out.

"Becca! What the hell?"

She dropped her gaze. "You'd better go."

"I can stay," James offered.

She rolled her eyes. "I'll be fine. Travis is ... Travis."

They stared at each other a second too long and Travis blasted the horn at them. James shot Travis a dirty look.

"You gotta convince Mr. Valcourt tonight," he reminded her, pedaling away.

Travis shut off the engine and jumped out. "What's that creep doing here?"

"The homeless guy was—" What had he done, really? He popped out from behind a tree and yelled at her, but it was hardly anything to report.

"Was *that creep* bothering you too? Jesus Christ, Becca. Maybe you oughta get a car."

Anger flared in her gut. "With *what* money, Travis?"

"Uh, I don't know. Ask your grandma. I asked my dad and look what I got."

He obviously couldn't tell by the worn-out shingles on the house or the cracked foundation that Becca and her grandmother were surviving on fumes. He couldn't see that his girlfriend studied hard because she needed to earn the best scholarships or that the reason why she worked her ass off all summer was to save up money for college. He didn't understand why money was a sore point for the St. James family, and if he couldn't understand now, he never would.

She wanted to dump him right then and there, but a part of her wanted him to understand. If she could just explain what was going on, then he could be a better boyfriend.

"I learned something today," she said. "My mom—"

Travis threw his arms around her, lifting her off the ground. "I just don't know what you're doing with that guy."

"I told you we've been studying."

He squeezed her. "You also told me you'd stop seeing him."

I did say that, but... "Travis..."

"It's fine," he said, letting her go. "I know you had to see him one more time to let him down gently. Guys like that have a hard time with hearing no. I get it."

Becca looked down. "I need to get changed."

"Yeah, you look all sweaty. But get a move on, because Mom's waiting and we're already really late."

She wanted to cancel. She wanted to dump Travis and invite James over to drink sour lemonade with her and Gran. But tonight was her chance to speak to Declan Valcourt and get her name taken out of the running. So she raced inside and got cleaned up.

Gran poked her head in to say hi just as Becca pulled on a pair of jeans and an oversized blouse that she tied at the waist. Then she topped off the look with a pastel pink headband.

"You look lovely, dear," said Gran. "Travis is sure going to love it."

But it wasn't Travis she was thinking of when she picked out her clothes.

"Thanks," she said, looking at Gran in her dresser's mirror. She thought about how easily Sadie let it slip about her mom's murder. Would Gran give up the same information as easily?

"What really happened to my mom?" she blurted before Gran turned away.

Gran blinked several times. Her eyes glazed over. "Honey? Are you feeling okay?"

Becca's throat tightened. "I just want to know."

"Oh, honey." Gran shuffled into the room and pulled her into a hug, rocking her back and forth. "What a strange question! I *am* your mother."

Becca froze. Chills raced down her spine. She couldn't move, couldn't think. Gran continued to rock her until finally planting a kiss on her cheek and patting her back.

"Now, go on. You don't want to keep Paul waiting."

Chapter 10

ecca hurried downstairs. She was relieved that Gran hadn't just revealed some devastating family secret, but felt frustrated and confused. *Who was Paul?* Her grandmother was losing it big time, and Becca didn't know what to do.

That was a lie. She knew, and it involved sticking the old woman in the Red Lion Retirement Village to live out her remaining years. The thought made her choke up. She wiped her eyes, careful not to smudge her mascara, as she entered the living room to meet Travis.

Except he wasn't there.

"Travis?"

She followed the sound of a muffled, low voice to the kitchen. Before marching in, she paused at the door and listened. He was on the phone, talking quietly, but she could still make out a few words.

"...probably somewhere across town... Just get that piece of shit, will ya?"

Becca poked her head in and cleared her throat. It was time to get this over with. Dinner with the parents and then beg Mr. Valcourt for her life. Then she would break up with Travis on Monday. It would all be over soon.

"Oh, hey," said Travis, catching sight of her. He muttered a goodbye to the person on the other end and fumbled to hang up the phone. "Sorry, just had to let my folks know we're running late."

"Didn't sound like you were talking to your folks," she pointed out.

"Were you *eavesdropping* on me? God, Becca, since when did you become so paranoid?"

Since I found out my mother was murdered and it might have something to do with the Harvest Festival. "I wasn't. I just caught the end of your call."

"Well, *that* wasn't them, okay? I called them first and then I called Heath. I wanted to tell him to keep a look out for that homeless asshole."

Becca crossed her arms. "You didn't tell him to go beat him up, did you?"

"Why not?"

"Because I don't want anyone to get hurt."

Travis caressed her arm, moving in close. "No one's gonna get hurt."

She held her breath. "Do you promise?"

He grinned, pulling her in for a hug. "Promise."

* * *

The Valcourt house stood on several acres of land on the edge of town. From their second-floor balcony, you could see Pigeon Lake, the sight of which brought Becca back to that embarrassing night when she tried to get Travis to have sex with her.

Though she had met Declan and Trish Valcourt several times over the summer, Becca still felt terribly uncomfortable in their lovely home. In Becca's mind, the Valcourts lived in a mansion that was too big and opulent to have been built in town, yet it was as if the reeve wanted his house situated on a hill overlooking the community so he could keep watch over everything.

When Travis and Becca entered the house, he took off both of their coats and hung them over the railing. "We're home!" he announced.

Trish Valcourt poked her head out of the kitchen. She wore a frilly apron and oven mitts, which she used to wipe her brow. Behind her, the hired cook plated the food.

"You're late!" Trish shouted back. This was a shouting house. Big house, big personalities, big voices. "Lucky for you, the dinner is taking longer than expected."

Travis clapped his hands and smiled at Becca. "See? Nothing to worry about."

Becca nodded, looking at the art on the walls and the statue of two marble lovers wrapped around each other in an erotic embrace. Her eyes lingered on it a little too long when Declan Valcourt sauntered out of his office, puffing on a cigar.

He pointed at the statue. "Beautiful, isn't it? Picked it up during our last trip to Venice. Really caught my eye."

"It's … nice," Becca squeaked.

"Can I offer you something to drink?"

"I-I don't drink," she said.

Travis laughed. "He means pop or iced tea, Becs."

"Um, maybe just water?"

"Is that a question or a request?" replied Mr. Valcourt.

"Water, sir."

He laughed, beckoning them to follow him into the dining room. He stepped behind a small, mirrored bar cart that was fully stocked with all sorts of whiskeys, rums, and vodkas. On the cart was a pitcher of ice-cold water. He poured one for each of the teens and then poured himself a whiskey.

"What a day," he said.

"Dad, my car's been making a funny sound," said Travis. "Like it's lost some of its power."

Mr. Valcourt frowned. "I'm sure it's fine, son."

"Can you take it to the shop for me?"

"Why can't you take it?"

Travis shrugged. "Then I gotta spend all day there…"

"And you would prefer *I* spend all day there? While juggling my business with my duties as reeve? Do you think so little of the work I do to provide for this family? Why don't you bring your homework with you? Seems like the best use of your time."

"But—"

Mr. Valcourt cut him off with a single look. "No buts. If you have a problem with your car, you deal with it."

"Dinner's ready!" called Mrs. Valcourt.

She pushed open the door that connected the kitchen and dining room. The cook carried steaming hot plates of mashed potatoes, vegetables, and beef smothered in a thick sauce. Once each plate was set on the table, the cook left.

Mr. Valcourt took his place at the head of the table with Mrs. Valcourt sitting opposite of him; Travis and Becca sat in between. Mrs. Valcourt had changed out of her apron and Becca could see that she was wearing a black, satin button-up shirt and her sandy blonde hair was perfectly coiffed atop her head.

Placing a cloth napkin in his lap, Mr. Valcourt snuffed out his cigar and declared, "Let's dig in." For the next ten uncomfortable minutes, Becca chewed and swallowed in the deafening silence of their family dinner. Every now and then Mr. Valcourt would make a moaning yummy noise to which his wife would smirk proudly.

When Becca dared look up from her plate, she caught Travis gazing at her. He winked.

She felt guilty — eating their food and accepting their hospitality — knowing she was going to end things with him.

Finally, when Mr. Valcourt had cleared his plate, the cook came in and cleared the table, including Becca's half-finished water. The food in her mouth slid slowly down her throat, and she hoped she wouldn't choke in front of them.

The cook returned with dessert. Panna cotta with cherry sauce. Mrs. Valcourt dipped her spoon into one corner of the creamy dish and licked a small bit off. Then she beamed at Becca. "So, tell me, Becca — are you excited for the festival?"

"Umm..." She glanced sideways at Mr. Valcourt. His face was as stony and unreadable as the marble lovers statue.

She wanted to talk about Harvest Queen, but not with an audience. She just wanted two minutes alone with Mr. Valcourt. Maybe with Travis getting her back.

Mouth full of panna cotta, Travis answered, "She doesn't wanna do it anymore."

Mrs. Valcourt's spoon clattered against her plate, masking the sharp sound of her gasp.

Mr. Valcourt picked up his napkin and placed it on the table, next to his untouched dessert. He leaned back in his chair, his tongue searching for food in his teeth.

All eyes were on Becca, burning through her skin and bones to get at the heart of her reasoning. *Why wouldn't she want to be queen for a day?* Becca stared at her lap and quietly said, "I just, uh, don't think I'm a good fit."

The tension at the table was palpable. Becca glanced at Travis for backup, but he was too busy shoveling dessert into his mouth to do anything more than stare at her.

Then Mr. Valcourt cleared his throat. "Becca, let's speak in my office."

She was relieved to leave the table and not have to look at Mrs. Valcourt's gaping mouth and stunned expression. She scurried out of the dining room and across the foyer, where her sneakers squeaked on the tile.

Mr. Valcourt's office was hidden behind a heavy oak door. The first thing he did after closing them in was to march straight toward a built-in bar. He seemed to have a bar in every room. He poured himself a drink, welcoming Becca to sit down on one of his two brown leather couches.

"Excuse the mess," he said, though she couldn't see any sign of a mess. Just a lot of stuff — books filling every shelf, portraits covering every bit of wallspace, a decadent mural of angels in heaven painted on the ceiling. Mr. Valcourt had a lot of wealth to show off.

With a drink in hand, he settled down on the opposite couch. He crossed a leg over his knee and took a sip of some brown liquid. "Now," he began. "What makes you think you're not a good fit?"

Toying with her hands in her lap, Becca had trouble looking at him. His eyes were just too focused, too intense. She had felt that way when Travis first introduced them. Back then, she figured he was sizing her up as an acceptable girlfriend for his son.

"I just don't think it's right for me," she said. "I've been doing a bit of research and—"

"Research?" He laughed, the sound booming through the office. He uncrossed his leg so he could lean in toward her. "You're a smart girl, but you know there's no essay-writing portion, don't you?"

"Yes, sir. I know."

He scrunched up his face. "I told you — don't call me 'sir.' It's Declan."

"Okay," she agreed, swallowing.

"I've seen this before, back when we had the Harvest Festival in '66," he said. "You're just getting cold feet."

"Sixty-seven," she corrected. "The date was changed because my mom got pregnant."

A frown briefly crossed his face, but like any politician worth his salt, he turned it into a smile. "You weren't kidding about doing your research."

She nodded. "And every girl who ever served as queen ended up dead. So you can see why I'd like to drop out."

Settling back on the couch, he nodded and swirled his brown liquid around. Two small ice cubes clinked together. "Dead? I don't think so."

"It's true," she said, wishing she had brought her notes. "It's very strange, but we were able to find information all the way back to 1916. None of the queens lived after."

"We? Has Travis been involved in this?"

Becca didn't see how that was relevant. "No…"

"Good."

"Good?"

"Yes, good. I don't want Travis wasting his time — *his precious homework time* — on wild goose chases, and I'm very disappointed in you, Becca. I thought you were smarter than that."

"But this is important. Someone might get killed."

"Your mother was Harvest Queen," he said. "She wasn't killed."

"Do you remember her?"

"Sure," he said. "She was a few years younger than me. Lovely, nice girl. But she wasn't killed. She was sick. Leukemia, wasn't it? Very sad. But that's proof right there that someone isn't going around killing young girls. Okay?"

Becca simmered under his steady gaze. She began to think her theory was stupid and immature. Of course there was no killer. The killer would have to be almost eighty by now. There was no way it was possible.

"I should go," she said quietly.

"I think that would be best." Mr. Valcourt stood up and polished off his drink before escorting her out of the office and to the front door. Then he called for Travis. "Becca's leaving. Come say goodbye."

"Mr. Valcourt," she said, "I'm really sorry for all your trouble. Again, I just don't want to be queen anymore."

"I understand," he said, shaking her hand. "But it's your civic duty. There's nothing to be afraid of." Travis wandered out of the dining room and Mr. Valcourt put an arm around both of them. "Make sure Miss Becca gets home all right, will you?"

"Sure, Dad."

Then Mr. Valcourt pinched her cheek between his knuckles and grinned. "We don't want anything bad to happen to our Harvest Queen."

Chapter 11

ames didn't like leaving Becca with that asshole Travis, but he didn't see any other way. Dinner with the Valcourts was her chance to quietly and gracefully drop out of the running. Once Becca was safe, then they could concentrate on how to present their findings to the town. Maybe the local newspaper would be interested? Or he could send a letter to the city paper? Should they bring in a lawyer? What kind of heat would they take for this? It was big, earthshaking news, and James didn't want any repercussions.

Whatever they had stumbled upon was going to change Morganville forever.

He gripped the handlebars of his bike as he flew home. The handlebars... He could still imagine Becca perched on them, wobbling against him. He knew he wouldn't have let her fall, but a part of him really wanted to feel her against him. The scent of her lilac shampoo under his nose drove him crazy the whole ride to her house.

It was killing him to be so close to her and not touch her all because that asshole Travis had his hooks in her. As soon as Becca was out of the race, James was going to ask her out. Travis be damned. All she had to do was say no and he would back right off.

Speeding home, he decided to take a shortcut through the church's park. Becca didn't have much luck last time. The drunk homeless guy was freaky, but James figured that, as a guy, he had nothing to worry about. Stories about men being grabbed and dragged into the bushes were unheard of, and this was a small town. Even if someone was killing off Harvest Queens, he doubted he would run into too much trouble.

So when a big, brutish figure blocked his path, James barely blinked. He steered onto an adjoining path. The homeless guy was one man. He couldn't catch him after a maneuver like that.

He glanced over his shoulder to see what the guy wanted when he crashed into the outstretched arm of another burly guy. He flew off his bike and landed on the cold, hard pavement, groaning.

The two big guys stood over him. As James straightened his glasses, he saw that no — there were actually three.

Did the homeless guy have friends? he wondered, before being hoisted up by his jacket collar. In the single lamplight, he recognized Heath, Chester, and Mark.

Travis's friends.

"Hey, city boyyy!"

Shit.

Heath threw the first punch. James's head snapped back. The hit cracked his lens. The other two jerks laughed. James tasted blood.

Heath hit him again and James slumped down. His head felt heavy. Chester kicked his legs out as if that would help. *Idiots*, he thought. *Stupid fucking idiots.* The thought made him chuckle. These three were stupider than him and yet they were kicking *his* ass, and all James could do was snicker, which pissed them off.

"Shut up, fuckface!" one of them snapped.

Heath pounded him again. This time stars exploded behind his eyes. He couldn't see through them — there were too many. He was drowning in stars. And there was yelling all around. So much yelling.

"Keep away from Becca!"

He wanted to lay down and go to sleep, but they wouldn't let him. Two of the bastards held him up. He tried to droop down, but they were big, strong farm boy types. Probably chucked hay bales and wrestled cattle for fun. James was nothing to them.

"Let him go."

Another voice. A man's voice. It was rough and scratchy, but it held water with the three boys. One of them let go and took off running. Heath punched James in the gut one last time, knocking the air out of him. James folded like laundry as he fell to the ground.

Head resting on the pavement as he gasped for breath, James thought he was going to die. He remembered an old trading card set he had as a kid — famous magicians. It said Harry Houdini died from taking a bad hit from a boxer. It was all James could think about as he felt his insides adapt to being rearranged by an asshole who wouldn't know his renal system from his rectum.

James coughed, spitting blood.

"Y'okay, kid?" The man shuffled over, but all James could see were his scuffed and worn Nikes.

James rolled over to see the homeless guy looking down at him.

Uh-oh…

* * *

Becca sat in silent shock the whole ride home. Travis went on and on about some high school drama shit, but Becca wasn't listening. Her brain kept replaying a list of names: *Millie Sawyer, Marsha McCreedy, Viola Pettit, Bethany St. James…*

Finally, he reached over and squeezed her leg. She jumped, which made him laugh. "Wow, that news really got you stunned, huh?"

"I don't want to be queen!" she shrieked. The sound of her strained voice startled them both and Travis pulled his hand away. She bit down on one of her knuckles and stared out the window as they drove.

They passed the library and the church grounds. Becca considered asking Travis to pull over. She would rather take her chances with a drunk homeless guy than... *No.* She didn't want to be out there either.

"Being queen sounds awesome," he said after a long silence. "You get all sorts of free stuff. Even a dress for the big event. And what about that scholarship? I thought that's what this was all about?"

"I don't want any of it. Not anymore."

"Wow," he muttered, shaking his head. "You're acting really ungrateful. My dad went to bat for you. The least you could've done is thanked him."

Becca's head throbbed. "No one's listening to me."

"I don't think you know what you want. First, you wanna be queen and then you don't. Like, make up your mind."

"I have!" She strained against the seatbelt. *"I don't want to be queen!"*

"Well, that's tough. You gotta do it now or—"

She snapped at him. "Or what?"

"Or you'll disappoint a lot of people."

She sank down. They were almost to her house. Shadows moved between the trees and stretched over fences. She decided to keep her mouth shut until she was safe at home. Then she would tell Travis that they needed to break up, and first thing in the morning, she would get her grandmother involved. There would be no Harvest Queen this year, if that's what needed to happen.

Travis stopped the car, resting his arm on the steering

wheel. He didn't bother to reach over to touch her. He just stared out the opposite window.

"I'm not gonna call you this weekend," he said.

"Fine," she shot back. "Don't call me ever."

"This is stupid," he said. "You're being immature. Maybe you'll see the light on Monday."

Doubt it. She got out and slammed the door.

The Firebird roared off as she stormed toward the house. She wished she had made it more official. *Travis, it's over.* That's all she had to say. *I think we should see other people.* That's a good one. *It's not you, it's me.* Classic.

But when it came down to it, he stunned her with his comment about "being immature." Becca didn't think she was immature. She was almost an adult. And yet, Travis had this incredible way of derailing her thought process.

Well, not anymore. It's over.

She stopped stomping her feet as she neared the house. She didn't want to wake Gran.

But then the silence was thick, and her ears began to play tricks. Was that the sound of late-season mosquitos zipping past her head? Was that highway noise in the distance? Were there footsteps behind her?

She looked over her shoulder. Mrs. Peck walked by with her two tiny dogs on a flowery pink leash. The woman gave her a friendly wave.

Relieved that it wasn't someone dangerous or creepy, Becca waved back and opened the screen door. That's when she heard the moan. She froze. *Someone is there!*

She put her back against the door so no one could jump her — and she spied a foot sticking out from one of the bushes.

And she recognized the shoe.

"James?"

He was curled up against the house, his jacket pulled over his face.

She bounded down the steps and squeezed through the plants, careful not to step on any of Gran's flowers. She crouched next to James, shaking his shoulder. He moaned again, lifting his head. Something dark and wet coated his mouth and nose. His right eye was swollen shut.

"Oh, my god," she breathed.

Chapter 12

*J*ames fluttered in and out of consciousness before realizing he wasn't at home. He was in someone else's bed. A cold, damp cloth slid off his forehead. His eyes blurred — *where are my glasses? Where am I?*

The walls around him were painted rose pink. The coverlet on the bed was edged in lace. The frilly lampshade on the wicker nightstand next to him was littered with a stack of books and a glass of water, and a photo of Travis Valcourt.

He groaned and tried to sit up. Becca was at his side in an instant. She sat on the bed, the too-soft mattress sinking under her weight as she joined him. He raised an eyebrow, which made his forehead hurt.

"What the—?"

She shushed him and then whispered, "My Gran's asleep. We have to be quiet."

He nodded, but that also hurt, so he settled back against the pillow and let Becca fuss over him with the cloth and a sandwich bag full of ice. He didn't hate the way she fussed over him. The glow of the lamp lit up her angelic, heart-shaped face, and cast a warmness in her rich, brown hair. He wanted to run his hands through it, but he felt too weak to do anything other than gaze at her.

"So what happened?" she asked.

What *did* happen? Head pounding, James collected his thoughts. "Got jumped by your friends."

"What friends?"

"Heath, Chester, … and that dumb-looking buzzcut guy."

"Mark."

"Yeah, that's the one."

"They're all pretty dumb looking to me."

He chuckled, which hurt his head even more. "Where are my glasses?"

"They were tucked into your pocket," she said. She reached over him, and for an instant James thought — *hoped and wished* — she was climbing on top of him. He wasn't sure what he would do if she did. He was too messed up to think straight.

But she wasn't putting any moves on him — she simply reached for his glasses.

He sighed when he saw the cracked lens. "Shit."

"Sorry," she said.

"It's not your fault."

Her lip trembled seconds before she burst into tears. She sat on the edge of the bed, covering her face as she struggled to sob quietly. Despite the throbbing in his skull and the pain in his lip, James sat up and patted her back. She twisted around and buried her face against his shoulder. He froze, catching a whiff of lilacs, before realizing she wanted to be held. He gently put his arms around her.

"Hey…"

"It *is* my fault," she whispered. "I thought… I thought I heard Travis telling them to beat up the homeless guy, but he sent them after *you*." She shuddered. Her tears soaked through his shirt. "I'm so sorry."

With all his mental strength, he detached her from his body so he could look her in the eye. "Hey, stop. It's okay. You didn't put out the hit." He grinned a little. "It's fine."

"It's *not* fine. Look what they did to you." She placed a cool hand on the side of his face.

James wanted to lean into it and let her take care of him, but he remembered something. "About that home-less guy… He saved my life."

"He did?" She took her hand away, disappointing him.

"He chased them away. Then he brought me here after I passed out."

Becca bristled. "He knows where I live?"

James grimaced. "Well, I kinda … told him? But then he took off with my bike… That was a dick move."

"He knows where I live. Great." She stood up, pacing

the room. "I don't want him to know where I live. He *hates* me for some reason. Why did you have to bring him here?"

"Look, I'm sorry," he said. "I wasn't thinking straight. And I'd rather be home in my own bed right now." Not true.

Becca rubbed her arms. From where she stood, James spotted his jacket hanging over her desk chair. He pointed to it.

"Can you hand me my…?"

She did and he went through the pockets. Out came a note on a ripped piece of newspaper and he handed it to her. "He gave me that."

Becca unfolded it. She stared at it, blinking several times. Then she gave it back to James. "I don't know what this is."

"I don't either, but look at the back."

I NEED TO TALK TO YOU was scribbled on one side. On the other was a badly printed news photo of a young woman. She almost disappeared into the black, smudged ink, but when Becca looked closely enough she could see—

"My mom."

"What do you think it means?"

Becca looked up. "I think it means the homeless guy knows something."

James sat up and swung his legs off the bed. She rushed over, pushing him against the mattress. "Where do you think you're going?"

"Home."

"You can't go home. What if those jerks come after you again?"

James knew that probably wouldn't happen. At least, not during the day. They were likely tucked away in their little race car beds, dreaming of beating up people. But he could tell something else was bothering her.

"What's wrong?"

"Nothing, I just—"

"Did you talk to the reeve?"

Lip quivering again, she nodded. Tears welled up in her eyes.

"Didn't go as planned, did it?"

She shook her head.

"It's okay," he said, pulling her down to lay next to him. He put an arm around her shoulder as she curled against him. His lips brushed her forehead. "We'll figure something out."

"Like my mom? She figured something out."

"She got pregnant, and she *still* had to be queen. It didn't change anything but the date." He swallowed, wondering if Becca had been considering getting knocked up. "Besides, you don't want to get ... you know ... pregnant over something like this. That's not a good idea."

Fire in her eyes, Becca sat up in a rush. "Are you saying my mom is stupid?"

"What? No—"

"She did what she had to do. She tried to save her own life. No one else would."

"I'm not saying she's stupid, but to bring a kid into this—"

Becca crossed her arms. "Well, she did. It's done."

"So what, you're gonna ask Travis to...?" He wished he hadn't said that.

"So what if I do?" she shot back.

His head started pounding again, more painful than before. "Look, we still don't know the whole story," he said. "So before you get yourself pregnant, maybe we should put together the rest of the puzzle?"

She sighed, uncrossing her arms. "Okay."

"Maybe you being queen could be a good thing. You're on the inside track now. You might be able to find out the truth."

"I don't like it."

"I know."

They stared into each other's eyes for a long beat. James felt their heads tipping toward each other. The mattress springs creaked. Her hand was on his. He was about to reach out to pull her in. His eyes began to close as his mouth parted to meet hers and then—

"Oh, my god — you're bleeding again." She sprang off the bed and ran around the other side. On the floor, she had a bowl of pink-tinged water and a dark rag.

James's stomach churned when he realized it was his blood. She had cleaned up his horrible mess of a face, and now the blood was swirling around in a bowl on the floor. *Jesus Christ.* He laid back down and touched his face.

"What did they do to me?" he moaned.

"I don't think your nose is broken, but your lip is split and you've got a real bad shiner." She dabbed gently under his nose, careful not to scrub his tender top lip. They gazed at each other again. "You still want to go home?" she asked.

"No," he said. "But what about your grandma?"

Becca smiled nervously. "We'll just keep this under our hats, okay?"

* * *

The next morning, Becca woke up stiff and cramped. A beam of sunlight hit her across the face, which was weird because her bed was positioned to be out of the sun's light in the morning, but then she remembered curling up on the floor so James could be comfortable in bed.

She sat up and watched him. He laid on his back with one arm over his head. His eyes were closed and he breathed like he was fast asleep, though his nose made a crackling, congested sound. She hoped those jackasses didn't break it. He was going to have a hard enough time explaining to his mom why he didn't come home last night, let alone why he looked beat to hell.

"James?" she whispered.

He grunted and rolled onto his side. She reached up to touch his back and wake him gently — just as Gran tapped on the door. Becca's heart jumped into her throat.

"Wake up, sleepy head!"

James and Becca both shot straight up and stared at the

door. Becca reacted first. She grabbed all the blankets and covered James as she climbed in on top of him. He stared at her wide-eyed, but there wasn't time to debate the ridiculousness of her plan. Becca couldn't get caught with a boy in her room.

Gran turned the doorknob and pushed. She poked her head in just as Becca pretended to sit up and stretch. "My, you're a late sleeper today! Who was in bed with you last night?"

James choked under the blanket. Becca kicked him, but drew Gran's attention by grabbing one of the books from her nightstand. She held up *Wuthering Heights*, and hoped with her poor eyesight, Gran couldn't see how flushed she looked. "Emily Brontë. It's really good."

"Oh!" said Gran. "That *is* a good one, and so is this!" She threw the door open and revealed a huge bouquet of red roses and baby's breath.

"Wow, Gran — who sent you that?"

Gran grinned. "It's not for me. It's for you."

Becca was too shocked to think up an excuse to get Gran to leave her room. Besides, the bouquet was bigger than the old woman's torso and the closer she got to the bed, the harder it was to see James's body hiding under the pile of blankets.

Her heart thundered — *can she hear it, will it give me away?* — and she started to sweat.

"What for?" she asked, reaching for the small white card jutting out of the center.

"You tell me," said Gran.

Becca opened the card.

I'm an idiot. Love, Travis.

"It's from Travis." She felt uncomfortable saying his name with James in her bed.

"How nice!" said Gran. "You caught a good one there. We should have him over for tea tomorrow."

"Sure, Gran," Becca said, willing to say anything to get her out of the room. "Lemme get dressed and I'll be right down. Can you put those in some water for me?"

"Of course," she said, shuffling back out of the room. "What a lucky girl you are."

Gran closed the door on the way out. Becca rested her head against her headboard. As soon as the coast was clear, James pushed the blankets off and stared at her. His face was as red as a tomato. "That was close."

"Yeah," she said, blushing furiously. She hopped out of bed and went to check that the door was definitely closed. "Let's not do that again."

He got up and found his jacket and glasses. He tried seeing through them, but gave up and tucked them in his pocket. "I'd better go. My mom's gonna flip out if she checks my room and I'm not there. Bad enough I'll have to explain why my face is messed up."

"I tried," she said, standing up. She wandered to the window and peered outside, not wanting to face James. But with the early morning flowers and Travis's name in the air, she felt she had to say something.

"You tried what?" he asked.

"I really did try to quit, but Mr. Valcourt…" She

glanced at him, watching his confused face give way to a pained smile.

"I know," he said, joining her at the window.

"I'm sorry."

He took her in his arms, turning her to face him. He needed her to know he was dead serious.

"You have nothing to be sorry about. It's going to be okay. I won't let anything happen to you. And the second things look bad, I'll steal my mom's car and we'll run away."

"What about your plan to graduate early?"

"Fuck it," he whispered with a smile.

Grabbing the lapels of his jacket, she kissed him. His hands slid down to the small of her back, pressing her warm body against his. She parted her lips to take a breath and they stared at each other.

"You were right — you have to go." She opened the window and popped out the screen. She explained that all he had to do was climb out onto the roof and grab onto the eavestrough. It wasn't that far to climb down. "You'd better hurry."

He moved slowly, but did as she asked. He was halfway out the window, when he turned back and smiled. He wanted to say something romantic or cool, but all he had was, "See you soon?"

"See you soon."

Chapter 13

ecca wanted nothing more than to lounge in bed all day, reading *Wuthering Heights* and daydreaming about kissing James. She wouldn't have guessed it from the look of him, but he was a great kisser. And the way he held her... Becca sighed as she pulled a clean shirt over her head.

But she didn't have time to daydream.

Downstairs, Gran was muddling about in the kitchen. The Saturday newspaper was spread out on the kitchen table. The featured story was about the upcoming Harvest Festival and what attendees could expect. The sidebar announced Becca as queen and that her coronation was next Saturday. She poured over every last word, as if there would be some hint as to how she was going to die.

She slouched down in her chair and Gran brought over

a plate of toast. "Gran, can you help me with something?"

"Like your posture? Sit up straight — your back will thank me later."

Becca straightened up. "I'm supposed to be Harvest Queen."

Gran's eyes crinkled. She glanced at the newspaper, but didn't say anything.

"I don't want to do it."

"Why not?"

She fidgeted. "I..."

Before she could even decide between lying or spilling her guts about everything, Gran reached across the table and held her hands. Tears welled up in Gran's eyes. "I said to stay out of it, and you didn't listen. Now it's too late. You have to do your civic duty."

Civic duty? Why does everyone keep saying that?

"It's a free country, Gran," she replied. "I don't have to do anything I don't want to."

Smack!

Gran's slap jerked Becca backwards, her chair screeched on the linoleum. She touched her cheek as a sharp sting set in. Gran had never hit her, nor had ever shown any violent tendencies. The suddenness of it took her breath away.

The old woman pushed her chair back and stood up. She marched to the sink, moving as if she were twenty years younger and not crippled by a bum knee and a stiff hip. She grabbed plates out of the dish rack and hurled them into the sink. They shattered into pieces, which she began to pick up and wash with a dry cloth. Then she dropped the broken pieces into the rack.

"You can be so *goddamn selfish* sometimes," she snarled. "I work hard to provide for you and this is the thanks I get. *'No, Mom, I don't want to be queen.'* It's all you've talked about for weeks! So what changed? Don't like the dress they picked out for you? Ungrateful little bitch."

Becca began to cry. If Gran was reliving some past argument with her mom, Becca felt her mom's fear. She covered her face, peeking through her fingers to watch the old woman bust more plates in the sink.

"You think Paul deserves a miserable girl like you? What a joke. No one's going to want anything to do with you. You're a selfish brat."

"I don't want to be queen," Becca whimpered, hoping the sound of her voice would bring her Gran back.

"Doesn't matter what you want. What's done is done. You've been chosen."

Suddenly the old woman stopped washing dishes. Wobbling on her feet, she grabbed the sink. Becca rushed over to steady her, but wasn't fast enough. Gran fell down, crying out.

They spent the rest of the day in the emergency room in St. Aubergine. Becca had to call an ambulance to take them into the bigger town, which had its own hospital, but when the paramedics arrived and told her there might not be room for her to ride with them, Becca cried her eyes out. "I don't want to leave my Gran."

So they squeezed her in and went to the hospital. Gran floated in and out and consciousness.

By Sunday, the old woman was taken into surgery to deal with her hip. It broke when she hit the floor, and Becca hated herself for not being able to catch her grandmother. When a nurse advised she go home for the night and come back in the morning, Becca nodded dumbly and wondered how she was actually going to do it. She hadn't brought any money for bus fare, and even if she had, the buses had stopped running for the night.

Staring at the bank of payphones, she wanted to call James, but couldn't remember his phone number; it was scribbled down in her notebook back home and the hospital didn't have a Morganville directory. Besides, he didn't have a car, and she wasn't sure how his mom would feel about making a late-night trip into town to help out the girl that got her son beaten up.

So she called the number she remembered so very well. Travis had written it on her wrist when he first asked her out. She didn't wash that arm for weeks, until the ink eventually faded away. She knew that number by heart.

Mr. Valcourt answered. "Becca! Nice to hear from you. I apologize for the way we left things the other night."

"Thanks." Her voice croaked. "Is Travis there?"

"Is everything okay? You sound upset."

"No, I just…" She covered the mouthpiece as she started to weep again.

"Do you need help?" he asked. "Where are you?"

"I'm at the hospital. My Gran fell and—"

"I'll be right there."

Becca had hoped Mr. Valcourt would have sent Travis. As angry as she still was, she felt more at ease with him than with his father. But no. Mr. Valcourt came alone in his maroon Chrysler LeBaron. He jumped out of the car, leaving it parked in the emergency vehicle spot, so he could come around to open her door.

She hesitated. "Do you think it's okay to leave my Gran? I left her a note, but—"

"She'll be fine," he said. "Travis can bring you back after school tomorrow."

Inside, the car smelled like smoke. The ashtray drawer was stuffed with butts and an open pack sat on the dashboard. As he pulled away from the hospital, he lit up a cigarette.

"Now what happened?" he asked.

She explained everything, leaving out the part where Gran experienced a break in reality. She didn't want him to misinterpret the moment as being evidence of Gran's true feelings about the Harvest Queen role. As soon as Gran felt better, Becca would ask her to talk to Mr. Valcourt about calling it off. Simple as that. Becca believed in the power of adults in protecting kids.

"Everything's going to be okay," he said as they drove on the long, dark highway back to Morganville. "I asked Trish to get our guest room ready. You can stay with us until Dottie is well enough to return home."

"I don't want to be any trouble."

"You're no trouble at all."

"Thank you, sir."

"I'm obliged to do everything I can for the Harvest Queen, so if you need anything at all, just ask."

She was about to bite her tongue, and then thought, *what the hell?* "I really don't want to be queen. Can you choose another girl?"

He didn't speak right away, but his throat made a deep rumbling sound. His knuckles turned white on the steering wheel. Becca thought he was going to ignore her, and so she sank into her seat, wondering what to say next, when he spoke up. "Town council chose you, Becca, out of all the other applicants, because you're a wonderful young woman. Special. You have so much potential and could go on to do many great things. We know we've made the right decision, so why are you questioning it?"

"Because the other queens are dead."

"Is that why?" He laughed, shaking his head. "We haven't had a festival in almost 20 years, and we don't have them regularly, no. I think the one before last was in the '40s? A lot happens over the years, and sadly, yes, people die. I think something else is bothering you."

"No, they didn't just die — they were *killed.*"

"Your mother wasn't killed. She had cancer. And where did you hear this awful rumor about people being killed?"

"Sadie Frances."

He took a long drag on his cigarette. "I'm going to have a little talk with Miss Sadie. She shouldn't be spouting off to a young, fragile mind such as yourself. It's not appropriate."

"Is it true though?"

Mr. Valcourt studied her. His dark brows stitched together. Then he turned back to the road. "Of course not. Don't tell anyone I said this, but Miss Sadie likes to shoot her mouth off."

Becca had never gotten that impression from her, but she let Mr. Valcourt believe what he wanted. "What can I do to get out of this?"

"You mean quit? Well, Becca, quitters never prosper. If you quit, we quit, the whole town quits, and the Harvest Festival is about succeeding in the face of hard times. Our town isn't doing well, and this festival brings so much joy to our residents and business partners. If we quit, we let everyone down. And I know you wouldn't want to do that. Not with a sizable scholarship up for grabs."

"I don't need the scholarship," she lied.

"You will if your grandmother doesn't leave the hospital," he said coldly. The lights on the dashboard cast a sickly green hue on his skin and defined every dark line and crease on his skin. He wore a permanent grimace, and in any other light, he was a distinguished man. But in this eerie glow as he drove well over the speed limit, he looked like a ghoul.

"What are you saying?"

"I don't know," he said. "Elderly people have falls all the time. Some bounce back. Others ... not so much."

Becca gripped the arm rest. She wished she hadn't left

the hospital, wished she hadn't left Gran all alone.

"If your grandmother doesn't leave the hospital, how will you afford tuition? Travis says you're interested in medical school."

"That's right," she said, absently.

"That's a costly endeavor, but I understand. You want to save lives. That's why you're such a remarkable girl. Because *you care*. And that's why the council and I voted to increase the amount of the scholarship."

"What?"

"I know you don't care for frivolous things like pretty dresses and spa days. You care about your future, just like I care about the future of our town. I think we'll make a much better team if you stop resisting being Harvest Queen. What do you say?"

Becca was only silent for a second, because in the time that Mr. Valcourt droned on about scholarships and about what kind of person he thought she was, Becca came up with a plan. James's words stuck in her head: *You're on the inside track now. You might be able to find out the truth.*

So Becca said, "Okay."

Chapter 14

𝓘t took hours for Becca to fall asleep. The Valcourt's guest room was finely decorated, like a hotel room she could never afford. The sheets were silk as were the spare pajamas Mrs. Valcourt left for her. She sweat through them after an hour asleep and woke up feeling too hot.

As she laid in bed, staring at the bland, popcorn ceiling, the weight of the weekend began to wear on her and eventually she drifted off to sleep.

She woke with a start to the sound of the door closing. She sat up stiff as a board, grasping at the slippery sheet to cover herself. A tall shadowy figure crept closer.

"Who's there?"

"Just me," said Travis. "Who else?"

He stood by the side of the bed in only his plaid pajama

bottoms. They hung low on his hips, revealing a trail of dark hair from his belly button down.

"Shouldn't you be getting ready for school?" she asked. He was going to be really late if he ended up driving her home first.

He climbed into the bed, positioning a knee between her legs. He pulled the sheets away from her, eyeing her up. "I'm not going to school."

"Travis…"

"I'm not. I'm gonna stay right here." Pressing his body on top of hers, he began kissing her neck. Her body responded with an excited tingle.

"What about your parents?"

"Dad's at work. Mom went into town. I have you all to myself."

As she squirmed to sit up, he grabbed her by the hips and dragged her back down. She cried out in surprise and then Travis kissed her on the mouth. It shut her up for a second until he started kissing his way down her body, unbuttoning the pajamas as he went.

"I thought you weren't talking to me," she said.

"I said I wouldn't call you over the weekend," he said. "Weekend's over now."

His mouth lingered on her breasts, and she had to bite her lip to keep from moaning. It felt good, but she couldn't give him the satisfaction. She was done with him. "Get off, Travis, please."

"Don't worry, baby. I'll get us both off."

She pushed him. "Stop it."

He slid a hand down her pants. "Tell me to stop now."

"You have to stop," she said. Her body tensed and her back arched as Travis worked his magic, and she wanted — needed — this so badly.

"You want it, don't you?" he teased.

She squeezed her eyes shut, nodding.

"Tell me you love me."

"What?" That request shocked her back to reality, and she tried to sit up.

"God, Becca," he panted. "You're so beautiful. I love you, baby. I wanna hear you say it. Say you love me."

"Travis—"

"Say it, baby," he crooned. "Say you love me."

Becca squirmed. It wasn't that long ago that she was begging for this moment — and now all she could think about was the damage Travis's asshole friends did to James all because of one phone call.

"Stop it." She pushed him off as she sat up, clutching the sheet.

Travis sat back. "What?"

"I don't want to do this anymore."

He threw his hands up with a big sigh. "Here we go. Tell me, Becca — what's your problem *now?*"

"Well, it's just that on Friday... I thought we were over," she said, sitting up and wrapping her arms around her knees.

"I don't remember breaking up with you."

"Well, I'm breaking up with *you.*"

His cheek twitched and he even smiled at her as he

processed this information. The smile had no humor in it and it chilled her to the bone. "Who the hell do you think you are?" He got out of bed and hiked up his pants. *"You* want to dump *me?"*

"You sent your friends to beat up James," she said, hugging herself tighter.

"No, I didn't."

"I heard the phone call."

"I told you — I wanted Heath to scare off that homeless shit bag for you. If the new kid got in the way, that's his fucking problem."

"You sent them on purpose. I saw what they did to him."

"Oh, yeah? You saw the new kid, did ya?"

Becca clammed up.

"You've got a thing for him, don't you?" He chuckled, scratching his brow. "This is just great. Fine, whatever. I can't believe I was going to fuck you just now."

Rolling her eyes, Becca climbed out of bed and quickly scooped up her clothes. "Why don't you go fuck yourself instead?" she muttered.

His nostrils flared and he pointed at her, about to say something he would regret, before shaking his head. He stormed out the door instead, shouting, "Get your shit and get out!"

Fine by me.

Becca walked home. It took almost an hour, but gave her time to think about how she could have handled that better. She had been in Mr. Valcourt's house, she could have accessed his office and dug up some dirt, but instead she had to push Travis away.

On the other hand, she was relieved to be done with him. He had been one more thing she didn't have time to deal with, not with Gran in the hospital indefinitely.

And then she worried that Mr. Valcourt's words could ring true. Gran might never get out.

When she got home, she called the hospital to find out how the old woman was doing. The nurse said she was in stable condition and wanted Becca to know that she was okay and not to miss school over it.

Becca smiled. That sounded like Gran.

But she decided to skip her classes anyway and try to get some sleep in her own bed. As soon as her head hit the pillow, she crashed hard.

She woke up around 8 p.m. to the phone ringing. It wouldn't stop, and for a while, she buried her head under her pillow and begged the caller to go away. But the ringing didn't stop. It had to be the hospital.

She jumped out of bed and ran down the stairs. She slipped on the bottom step, recovering before she could fall, and swung into the kitchen to answer the phone breathlessly. "Hello?"

"Becca, where've you been?" It was James. "I was worried sick."

Head clouded with sleep and all sorts of foggy dreams, she caught her breath. "What're you talking about?"

"I tried calling you this weekend and you weren't picking up the phone. I thought maybe I ... maybe I did something wrong? And then you weren't at school today. I was starting to worry."

As good as it was to hear his voice, his questions reminded her about her weekend from hell. "Gran's in the hospital."

"Oh, shit. I'm so sorry. What happened?"

"She fell. I was talking about Harvest Queen and she flipped out. And then she fell. I couldn't catch her—" Tears spilled silently down her cheeks, and she squeezed the phone so hard that her hand began to cramp.

"It's going to be okay."

"It's all my fault. I shouldn't have even entertained this whole stupid queen thing. I should have been like you and just focused on school. Now my Gran is in the hospital and you're never going to graduate early and I'm going to die."

"I'm coming over."

"No," she said. "It's okay. I'm just venting. I'm just scared."

"I know," he said.

Becca couldn't bear the weight of it, so she steered the conversation toward something she could grasp. "What did your mom say when she saw you?"

"I don't think I could repeat those words over the phone," he said. She could hear the smile in his voice. "Did you know my mom is a foul-mouthed sailor? Goddamn."

Becca winced. "Sorry."

"That's not the worst part. She caught me sneaking in

and screamed at me for over an hour. She said I'm grounded if I ever do that again"

She sucked a breath between her clenched teeth. "Double sorry."

"Yeah, but it was worth it," he said wistfully.

The hum in his voice made the back of her neck tingle, and she felt a blush coming on.

"I'm probably going to miss your coronation on Saturday, but I'll try to sneak out."

"You don't have to. Besides, if you get caught *again*, then what?"

"I'm not going to let you go through this alone," he said. "We don't know what we're up against yet."

He kept saying *we* like it was something they would both experience. He wasn't queen. He wasn't going to die or be killed or whatever the hell it was that the Harvest Queens had to go through. He would be just fine, like all the other boyfriends or love interests of the past queens.

Like Paul, whoever that was.

"Have you done any more research? Anything new to share?" she asked.

"Nothing yet. I think I've exhausted the library's resources."

Stretching out the phone cord, Becca stepped out into the hallway. She looked up the stairs, where the light tapered off into blackness. Gran's room. "Can you hang on? I just want to check something."

"Sure, what's—?"

She set the phone down on the counter and raced back

upstairs. She flipped on the hallway light and went into Gran's craft room. It was still an "organized mess," as Gran would call it, but the hope chest no longer had random projects stacked on it. As if Gran had recently gone through it.

Talking about Harvest Queen stuff must have dredged up memories for her, prompting the old woman to go through the chest.

Kneeling down, Becca opened it. She expected to find everything just where she had left it. She was wrong. So wrong. Everything that had been neatly put away was torn and shredded. It looked like someone went mad. A pair of scissors had been thrown on top of the mess. The one thing Becca had come for — the yearbook — was in tatters.

She picked it up by its broken spine. A few loose, crumpled pages drifted out. She flipped through to find her mom, but Bethany St. James had been scribbled over with a black marker. As Becca tried to make sense of this horrible mess, she flipped through looking for someone.

A boy named Paul.

Too many pages were missing or destroyed, and finally she closed it and threw it back into the chest. Frustrated, she hurried back downstairs and picked up the phone.

"Are you still there?"

"Yeah, what's wrong?"

"Can you do something for me?" *On top of all the other things you've done for me.*

"Anything."

"Do you still have my mom's yearbook?"

"It's back at the library at school, but I can get it first thing tomorrow."

"Good. Can you check to see if there are any guys in there named Paul?"

"Sure, why? What're you thinking?"

"I'm thinking there might be someone else who knows what really happened to my mom."

Chapter 15

The next day, as James scarfed down his dry toast at breakfast, his mother marched into the kitchen and made an announcement.

"Lucky you. No school this morning. I got you an appointment with Dr. Lee."

"Why?" he asked, mouth full of crumbs.

"What do you mean why?" By the way she hooked her fingers into the belt loops of her jeans, James could tell she was on edge. "You need new glasses. If you keep squinting at your homework, you're going to give yourself a migraine."

"But I just need glasses. Why do I have to see Dr. Lee? It's going to take all morning."

"So going to a school you keep telling me you hate is suddenly more important than your vision?"

Today wasn't a good day for taking a trip into the city. He promised Becca he would find that yearbook. But he kept his mouth shut.

His mother could read him like a book, and his silence told her that he didn't want to go. "You know, James, I have a lot of work to do and the last thing I want to do on a Tuesday morning is buy you new glasses. Do you know how much they cost? I don't have any vision coverage. This all comes out of our savings. Our *meager* savings, which is impacted by me not being able to work today. Can you see how inconvenient this is?"

James grumbled that yes, he could see and that he was sorry. What he wished he could have said was that a girl's life was hanging in the balance and he would gladly go without glasses for the rest of his life if it meant Becca would be safe.

The wait at Dr. Lee's office was ridiculous. As usual, the optometrist overbooked himself and James had to sit around flipping through water-damaged copies of *Reader's Digest* to keep entertained. *I should've brought a book*, he kept telling himself. Meanwhile, his mom took over the little kids' play table and went over some bookkeeping tasks while they waited.

Once Dr. Lee examined him and revealed that — *surprise, surprise* — his prescription was exactly the same, James still had to walk around the store with an optician and his mother as they told him what shape of glasses would best suit him.

I don't care.

He cared a little more than he thought, because they kept passing him frames that were just too big for his face. His cheekbones didn't need to see, so why did some frames cover half his face? He liked his old glasses, and unfortunately there were very few pairs like his old ones that were in his mother's price range.

Finally, Mrs. Martin threw her hands up and slapped them against her jeans. "I don't know with you, mister. You're being awfully picky today."

"I don't want to do this."

"You don't want to *see?* Because that's what you're telling me when you say that."

His mom, like most concerned mothers, loved to throw around crazy phrases like that.

"Fine," he said, dragging his feet back to the wall of men's frames. He pointed at one pair in the clearance section. They looked like something Clark Kent would wear: Slightly oversized with a tortoiseshell pattern. His mother and the optician complimented him on the choice and how nice they would look with his hair and complexion, blah blah blah. His mother patted herself on the back for the price, which came in well below the amount she budgeted.

It was after lunch by the time James was at school. He didn't have any free periods and had to sit through lecture after lecture until it was finally 3:15 and he could run to the library.

He rushed inside, just about knocking over two annoyed-looking girls. The librarian made a face, but welcomed him in. He went over to her perch at the counter and asked if he could see the yearbook collection. "Specifically anything from 1964 to 1966?"

"An unusual request," she said, adjusting her glasses. "Take a seat, I'll bring over what I can find."

James chose the long table near the back of the library. Not too many students ventured this far back unless the place was full during a study period, and even fewer hung out in the library after school ended, so it was a peaceful wait — until Travis Valcourt barged in.

He had a single textbook under his arm and a pencil tucked behind his ear. At first James thought he was looking for a place to study, but then their eyes locked. Travis was on a seek-and-destroy mission.

Travis slammed his book on the table and pulled out a chair. He spun it around and sat on it backwards like he was one of those "cool" teachers. "Hey, man."

"Hey," James replied in a small voice. Shrinking down in his seat, he didn't want to antagonize Travis. He couldn't even stand to look him in the eye, afraid that Travis might somehow be able to read the guilt he now felt for kissing a much bigger and bolder guy's girlfriend.

"Nice shiner." Travis reached out to poke him in the face and James lurched backward. "Hey, man, easy. I don't wanna hurt ya." Leering, he leaned in close. "Or maybe I do."

What does he know? James wasn't going to let Travis bully him away from getting his hands on those year-books.

"What? Not gonna talk? Too good for me?" Travis straightened up, and for one hopeful moment, James thought ignoring him had worked and he was going to leave. Instead, Travis turned to look up at the librarian, walking toward them with an armful of yearbooks. He stood up to assist her, flashing his widest, most charming smile. "Hey, can I help you with those?"

She blushed and offered him the books. James's heart lodged in his throat. He didn't want Travis to get his grubby mitts on them.

"Thank you, Travis," said the librarian.

"Any time," he said, with a wink.

The older woman hurried off with an extra bounce in her step. Travis continued to grin even as he turned his attention back to James.

What a sleaze.

James reached for the top book — *1966* — but before he could get his hands on it, Travis snatched it away. "Come on…"

Travis flipped through it disinterestedly. What if he saw Bethany St. James? Would he make the connection? Was he smart enough to do that?

"I know you've been hanging around my girl," he said.

"What girl?"

"Don't play dumb," Travis snapped, sitting back down. "If you think you've got a chance with Becca, you're out to lunch."

"I think that's up to Becca," James replied, his pulse pounding.

Travis glared at him, chuckling coldly. "Becca doesn't know what she wants."

"I know she wants you and your dad to leave her the hell alone."

"I want *you* to leave her the hell alone," he replied. "I think you're putting crazy ideas in her head."

"Like what?"

"Like she's gonna die if she's queen. That's bullshit."

"How do you know? I've been doing a lot of research and—"

"Fuck your research, man. It's all bullshit. Nobody wants to hurt anybody."

"Somebody does," James insisted. "Somebody has been killing these girls since this town was incorporated and Becca is on the chopping block. If you care about her, don't you think you should do something? At least say something to your dad?"

He was surprised Travis let him get all his words out. If he actually listened would be another shocker.

James kept his eyes on the yearbook, which Travis slid under his textbook.

"She dumped me," he said.

Fighting the urge to smile, James tried to play it cool. He would have liked to jump out of his seat and pump his fist in the air.

"So what?" was all he said.

"So it's all because of you, isn't it?" The two young men stared each other down for several long, agonizing seconds. James finally had to blink and look away, because Travis was right. Travis leaned in until he was close enough for James to feel his breath. "Well, just remember — I was there first."

James wasn't an action hero type of guy, though he did want to punch Travis in his perfect nose. He looked down at the table and thought about leaving.

"That's right," Travis continued. "She fucked me. Yesterday morning. Right before school like a good little girl."

Action hero or not, James leaped up and raised a fist.

Travis leaned back. "Whoa, boy!"

"You leave her alone!"

Travis grinned like an idiot. He didn't say a word as the librarian hurried out from behind the counter to see what the outburst was about. "Young man," she said to James, "if you can't restrain yourself, I'm going to have to ask you to leave."

"I didn't—"

Travis had dropped the smile from his face. "He said some pretty hurtful things about my girlfriend. I don't feel safe in my own school. May I be excused?"

"You son of a—" James lurched toward him, but the librarian's icy glare froze him.

"Calm yourself, or I will call the principal!"

"Bye, James. Thanks for the book recommendation." Travis held up the 1966 yearbook as he slipped out.

James slumped back down in his chair. Seeing the young man deflated was enough to placate the librarian, who returned to her duties. Nobody becomes a librarian to break up fights.

He slouched down until he could rest his head against the chairback. Travis had slept with Becca — *after their kiss!* — and then took off with the book he needed. James wouldn't have been surprised if he sic'd his friends on him again.

He stared hopelessly at the 1964 and '65 yearbooks. Becca asked him to do her this favor and then she turned around and had sex with *Travis.*

Fuck the both of them.

She doesn't owe me anything, he thought miserably. *We weren't anything. Just two people who kissed. She had a boyfriend. What did I expect? That she'd run off and dump him?*

Travis said she did *dump him though.*

James picked up the 1965 book and flipped through it. He didn't feel like following through on his promise to Becca, but he was still curious. Something about a guy named Paul...

He found a couple of Pauls. It was a pretty common name in the province, but it was Paul #4 that made James take notice.

I know this guy.

Chapter 16

E rin and Candace joined Becca at Sassy's Salon. As part of her queenship package, Becca was permitted to invite two friends or family members to join her to get her hair and nails done. Becca would have preferred to skip the whole thing so she could have more time with her grandmother in the hospital, but on Friday she was again reminded of her "civic duty."

Though she didn't have her license yet (Gran was in the middle of teaching her how to drive, so Becca already knew a few things), Becca drove very carefully into St. Aubergine to visit. She parked far enough from the hospital so she wouldn't get a ticket and hoofed it inside, but once she got to Gran's room, she was surprised to see Declan Valcourt standing over Gran's bed.

"What're you doing here?" she asked, hackles raised.

He smiled and invited her to take a seat. Becca didn't need him to tell her where or when to sit, but she sat anyway, not wanting to make a scene.

"I wanted to check on Dottie," he said. "You haven't returned any of my calls."

"I don't have an answering machine."

"I can get you one, you know. I told you, I can get you anything you want or need because—"

"Because I'm the Harvest Queen," she mimicked. "I remember. The only thing I want is to be let out of my obligations."

"I told you, that's not possible."

Becca crossed her arms. "Seems like there are a lot of rules about being queen I don't know about. Mind sharing any of them with me?"

"When the time comes," he said.

She reached over to hold Gran's hand. The old woman dozed, oblivious to their conversation.

"I'm aware how frustrating this can be," he said. "I want to get it over with and go back to normal as much as you do. But I cannot stress enough how important it is for you to play ball here."

"Oh, yeah?"

"Your grandmother's life may depend on it."

She squeezed Gran's hand, wishing she would wake up and her hip would be fully healed, and that she could jump to her granddaughter's defense. But Becca would need a miracle for that to happen. Gran looked so frail and tiny under her sheet.

"Are you threatening us?" Becca asked.

"Of course not," he replied. "I'm on your side. I'm merely *warning* you. As long as you fulfill your duties, I will do everything in my power to ensure your grandmother is well taken care of."

"And if I don't?"

He studied her before he spoke, chewing on the inside of his cheek. "Then I can't say what could happen."

A regular politician. He had all the answers, but none of the transparency.

Becca would have to play along until she and James figured out the truth, and she was more determined than ever to get to the bottom of whatever was really going on with the festival.

The trouble was she hadn't heard from James since Monday night, and she hadn't been able to track him down at school. He hadn't shown up to any of the classes they shared, nor was he anywhere to be found. None of her friends claimed to have seen him. It seemed like he was avoiding her.

After the disturbing hospital visit, she called James's house to find out what was going on and to give him an update. And to remind him about the coronation on Saturday, though how could he forget? It was odd that they hadn't been in touch in so long, and she was starting to worry that something had happened to him.

Mrs. Martin answered the phone. "Oh, hi, Becca. How are you?"

"I'm okay, I guess," she said. "Is James around?"

"Uh… No, actually. He said he would be at the library. You could try there?"

"Okay, thanks."

Rather than run down to the library, Becca called first. Mr. Handy was there as usual. "Uh, I don't see him. I don't think he's been in all week."

In between her preparations for the coronation event on Saturday — which was the week before the festival launched — Becca kept calling and asking around. It only added to her nervousness about not being at the hospital with her grandmother. She doubted Mr. Valcourt would pull the plug on Gran, but there was enough weirdness about everything right now, that Becca couldn't be certain of anything.

So at Sassy's Salon late Saturday morning, while Candace and Erin gossiped about the other girls at school who lost out on being queen, Becca stared at herself in the mirror. Sassy's owner and primary hairdresser, Cyndy Mallon, stood behind her and played with her hair.

"You got a nice head o' hair on ya," she said, smoking a cigarette at the same time, though she was careful not to flick any ash onto her client. "They gonna crown you?"

"I don't know."

She sighed. "Somebody should've told ya. Would make my job a lot easier…" She grumbled the rest of her complaints. Becca didn't care. *Do whatever you want.* She was busy trying to keep her nausea at bay. Cyndy leaned down and looked Becca over. "You're lookin' a little green, hun."

"Ew," said Erin, leaning over to see what was wrong and to collect some kindling for the gossip mill. "You sure you're gonna make it to this afternoon?"

Becca pictured Mr. Valcourt standing over Gran's bed and the way he smirked at her. "I'll be there."

* * *

That afternoon, Erin and Candace linked arms with Becca and guided her into the community hall across the street from the Red Lion. Luckily, the hall was also close to home, so she could run over there right after to pick up Gran's car and head back to the hospital. Erin and Candace kept talking about an after party at Heath's house, but Becca had already committed to weaseling out of it.

"Becca, your hair is *so* pretty," said Candace.

Erin reached over and tugged on one of the loose curls that dangled down from the sides of Becca's updo. "You look like a princess. Totally."

"She's not a princess — she's the Harvest Queen," corrected Candace. "How does it feel?"

"Feels great," she said through gritted teeth. To say anything else would hurt Erin, who had desperately wanted the gig. *Wish I could trade you*, she thought.

"Your dress is super pretty too," added Candace. "Even though I don't think anybody should wear white after Labor Day."

Becca forced a smile as she looked down at the white,

cotton dress, paired with a jean jacket and her white sneakers, that might have been more suitable for a BBQ.

"Why? Is it bad luck?" asked Erin, opening the door.

Good luck. Bad luck. What did it matter anymore? Becca walked in, leaving the two friends behind to squabble over appropriate autumn clothing colors, and was instantly overwhelmed by the amount of people gathered inside. Refreshments were being served at the back of the auditorium and there was a long line of people with cash in hand.

Becca paused, staring in at everyone.

The girl at the table snapped her bubble gum. "It's fifty cents an entry," she said.

"For what?" asked Becca, caught naked without a purse.

The girl rolled her eyes. "You wanna watch the coronation, right? Well, max capacity is three hundred people and Reeve Valcourt says the whole town's gonna wanna show up to see the queen."

"I am the queen," she said.

"She's the queen," Erin and Candace affirmed. Then Candace added, "She doesn't have to pay, does she?"

The girl looked back and forth between the three of them. "Uh, I don't know."

"That's no," decided Candace, who also decided that included herself and Erin. They marched Becca past the front table and entered the auditorium.

Becca looked around. People were taking their places in folding chairs. The stage had been decorated as it usually was for graduations or weddings. And on a small table next to the podium, where Mr. Valcourt sound-checked the microphone, sat a white, silk pillow — on top of which sat a sparkly tiara.

Erin elbowed her excitedly. "Guess what? Tiara!"

Knees weakening, Becca sat down in one of the folding chairs at the back of the auditorium. "Cool."

"What's the matter?" she asked.

"She's getting emotional," said Candace. "It's all happening so fast. It's her big day."

"Oh," said Erin.

Becca saw James sitting in the opposite section next to his mom. He wore a new pair of glasses that looked really good on him. Their eyes met, and then Erin sat down, blocking Becca's view. She lowered her voice and asked, "Um, you don't really want to sit *here*, do you?"

"Uh, no," Becca said, agreeably. Being agreeable to everything might be her only way to make it through the day. "I just want to rest for a second. Candace is right. It's a lot to take in."

"Good," she snorted. "Because the new guy is staring at you. What a creep, right?"

"He tried to beat up Heath last week," said Candace, regaling them with the story as if she hadn't regaled them and everyone else at school with it all week. "Thank god Mark and Chester were there to help."

I bet. Becca nodded agreeably.

"Do you think Travis will show?" Erin said with a grin.

"Probably," said Candace, checking her nails. "Becca looks amazing. He'd be stupid not to show."

She peered over Erin's shoulder. James was looking down at his shoes, his legs stretched out. It was time to exercise one of the perks of being Harvest Queen. "Hey, could you guys get me something to drink?"

Candace snorted. "The line is too long."

Becca smiled. "Oh, come on. It won't take a minute. Please? I'll pay you back."

She sighed, but stood up and kicked Erin's foot. "Come on. Let's go."

Erin sighed too. "We'll be right back. Don't let that creep bug you. If I see Chester, I'll send him over to protect you."

"Thank you," said Becca.

As soon as the two wandered off toward the refreshments line, Becca knew she didn't have much time. She stood up and stared at James until he finally looked her way again. Then she nodded toward the door, beckoning him to follow as she exited the auditorium.

She glanced back. He was a few feet behind her when a group of people separated them. But he wasn't far behind. She turned down the dimly lit hall and headed for the utilities room.

The door was unlocked and she let herself in. "Anyone here?" she called out. The hall had a janitor, but he was rarely on site until after the events. Becca didn't want to take any chances, however. "Uh, I think there's a big mess at the refreshment stand and—"

No one was there.

She flicked a switch, which lit up a bare light bulb. She wandered in, rubbing her arms. It was chilly, like the air conditioning only worked in this one area of the building. She didn't want to be there any longer than necessary.

Come on, James. I need you.

She stared at the ancient furnace system with its iron grate of a mouth, and decided if that thing roared to life, she was going to run for it.

The door slammed. She jumped, spinning around with a hand to her heart. "You scared—"

It wasn't James.

The homeless man blocked the door. Becca's heart stopped.

And then he locked her in.

Chapter 17

*J*ames felt righteous in his anger on Tuesday. Becca didn't deserve his help. Not if she was going to run back to her jackass boyfriend. But by Wednesday, the discovery he made in the yearbook began to gnaw at him. He tried to put it out of his mind. It wasn't information that was going to help him graduate early, and that's what he needed to focus on.

Getting the hell out of Morganville.

By Thursday, he began to have a change of heart. His pride was the only thing stopping him from being a decent friend and calling her. It still hurt too much — the thought of Travis with her. *Touching her.* And then he would remind himself that she supposedly dumped the jerk, so there was more going on than he was privy to.

And then Friday hit. His mother took him out of class

early to pick up his glasses. As soon as he got home, he tried calling Becca's house. No answer. So he went for a walk. Even found himself at her doorstep. No one was home.

He walked down to the burger place and treated himself to an ice-cold root beer. He lingered in one of the back booths, listening to happy couples giggle and chat, until the assistant manager asked him to leave because it was closing time. Then he went home and crashed.

The next morning, while he was trying to eat his breakfast and get some homework done, his mom broke the news to him. "Get ready. We're going to that coronation thing today."

"Why?"

"Didn't you hear? Your friend, Becca, is being named queen of that big festival happening next week."

Mom stuck the day's newspaper between him and his book. Becca's face was on the front page. Even though her photo was in black and white, he could still envision the ocean blue of her eyes. The sight of her almost made him choke on his cereal.

"I thought you'd want to go."

"Why?" he muttered, pushing the paper away, but making a mental note to dig it out of the trash later so he could see her again.

"I would've thought you'd want to support her. She seems like a very sweet girl."

"You only think she's sweet because she was nice to me that one time."

"She's always polite on the phone. She called last night when you were out. I thought maybe you were meeting up with her."

James dropped his spoon on the table. "She called?"

"She said she was looking for you. It was a little late, but you were already out..."

"Did she say what she wanted?"

"I don't know, dear." Mom patted his back. "Why don't we go this afternoon and you can ask her?"

James's mom only wanted to go so she could network with the other people there. She wore a blazer and brought a stack of business cards with her, but when it came time to shake hands and introduce herself, she quietly sat at the back of the auditorium and waited for someone to approach her. James felt bad, but also justified. His mom wanted to move here for her business. If she wanted to make it work, she would have to figure it out herself.

As he sat next to his mom, thinking about how he was going to tell Becca about what he found out, Becca walked in. Trailing her were those two insufferable girls, Erin and Candace. But it was Becca he couldn't take his eyes off of. She looked like a western-style angel in her denim jacket and white dress, with her long hair done up. James kicked himself for avoiding her for so long.

Stupid.

Whatever she'd had with Travis was over. They probably didn't even sleep together.

And then, after a few moments of talking with her friends, Becca stood up and stared at him. She wanted something. She wanted *him.*

She left the auditorium and he followed. Or tried to. A bunch of people blocked his path and she got too far ahead of him. She glanced back and then she was gone. James thought he lost her.

He pushed his way out to the greeter table and planted his hands on his hips. *Where did she go?* There was no trace of her.

He adjusted his glasses. There was a smudge on the left lens. He took them off and wiped them with the bottom of his t-shirt before holding them up to the light to check again. Out of the corner of his eye, he saw the homeless man sneak down the hallway and let himself into a room marked UTILITIES – STAFF ONLY.

James put his glasses back on and went after him. Before he could follow him in, the door slammed in his face. A second later, he heard a click. He grabbed the handle and pushed, but the door was locked.

* * *

Becca backed away from the homeless man without knowing what he wanted. Money? Rape? Chaos? Revenge for what happened the other week? All of the above?

She clutched her jacket closed over her chest. "Let me out," she said as calmly as she could manage as he came closer and closer. She didn't want to upset him or make a scene. Not today. Not when she promised to "play ball."

He slurred something, half-heartedly pointing at her. When he was near enough to grab her, Becca shrieked and jumped back. She crashed against the furnace.

Someone began banging and shouting on the other side of the door, and she prayed it was James. "Help!" she screamed, attempting to dodge around the man, but he scooped an arm around her waist and carried her farther into the room until she was lodged behind the furnace. He clamped a dirty hand over her mouth.

"N-now ssshut up," he hissed. His blue eyes glared at her intensely. His breath reeked of booze and years of dental neglect. "I jusss wanna talk to you…"

Squeezing her eyes shut, she shook her head and tried not to cry.

"You gonna be quiet a sec?"

Slowly, fearfully, she opened her eyes. His forearm pressed against her chest, keeping her pinned to the cold, hard wall.

"I'm not gonna hurt ya. Your friend— He give you my note?"

The torn photo of her mom. Becca nodded.

"Good." He removed his hand and arm, taking a single step back.

Becca darted around him, but this time she didn't get far. He had her by the elbow and threw her back against the wall. It knocked the breath out of her, and she slumped down to sit on the floor.

"I didn't wanna hurt ya," he said. "I jusss wanna talk. Will you lemme talk?"

Becca stared at him with wide, watery eyes. He inter-
preted her silence as an affirmative answer and started
pacing back and forth. He ran his hands through his
stringy hair in between wiping his runny nose on the back
of his hand.

"I-I knew yer mom." He stopped and let out a groan.
"Ughhh. I can't… My head's all… I can't get my thoughts
and words… It's *hard.*" He looked at his trembling hands.
"I jusss need a drink…"

Becca wasn't going to let him off that easily. If he was
going to trap her in this room and threaten her, then he
wasn't going to run off for a beer and leave her hanging
with a comment about her mom.

"My mom knew a lot of people. What makes you so
special?" she baited.

"She was my girl." He reached into his pants pocket,
fumbling around inside until Becca thought he might
expose himself to her. Probably some sick fuck who gets
off on tormenting young girls about their dead relatives.
But he didn't whip out his dick; he offered her a folded
photo instead.

It was a photo of her mom and a much younger,
cleaner version of the homeless guy. He was almost kind
of cute. He had a perfectly coiffed helmet of hair and
neatly trimmed sideburns. His arm was slung over her
mom's narrow shoulders. They were both grinning like
idiots in love. Scribbled on the back of the picture was
Summer '66.

That was supposedly around the time Bethany started

getting sick. She looked perfectly healthy. More proof that her mom's illness was fabricated. But what for? It had to be a coverup for the truth behind the Harvest Festival.

"Paul?" she asked tentatively.

He nodded slowly.

She handed the photo back. "What do you know?"

"More than I wanna remember."

"Tell me."

"Becca!" It was James. He was there to save her. If he barged through the door, the homeless guy might run away and she wouldn't have learned anything.

"Tell me!" she ordered.

"I-I-I need money."

"What? I thought you needed to talk? Now you're holding out on me?"

"I need help."

"I don't have any money."

He grumbled, turning his back on her and shuffling to the door.

She got up. "That's it? That photo looks like you cared about my mom. And you wouldn't trap me in here just to show me a picture. If you want to help her, tell me what you know."

"She's dead. No one can help her now."

"You can help *me.*"

He glanced at her, but wouldn't look her in the eye. "Money?"

"I can get you money. I-I'll ask someone."

"Lots?" He leaned against a wall and rubbed his head.

"I gotta leave town."

"I'll get what I can. Now tell me what you know about my mom."

"Harvest Queen," he said. "Back then, just like you."

I know that. She wanted to press him to hurry up, but she had a feeling he needed to take the long route down memory lane.

"She didn't wanna do it, but her mama made her. Told me she found out something bad. I didn't know what to do. I was just a kid."

"What did she find out?"

"Dunno. Never told me shit, and then a month before, she kinda just stopped talkin' about it, so I figured she got worked up over nothin'. And that's about when she asked me to do it."

"Do what?"

"Do *it.*" He shyly looked away.

Ew.

"I thought we were careful, but just before the festival, she came and told me she was knocked up. I said it wasn't mine, but all guys say that. I had a *future...*"

More banging on the door. More people trying to get in. Becca figured she and Paul didn't have much time left. Anyone who barged in now would scare him away. She had to tread carefully, but get him to hurry up. "So what happened?"

"I told her to get one of those ... you know ... *procedures.* I know it's a sin, but we weren't cut out to be *parents.* And then her mama and the council found out and that caused a whole thing. Can't have a big, fat, knocked-up Harvest Queen, they all said. Which didn't make any sense 'cause she was hardly showing."

"So they postponed it."

"Right. And a few months later, Beth skipped town. She asked me to take her, but I didn't want to get caught up in her drama. We were eighteen. I'm no dad." His eyes watered. "She begged me though. Called me every night before she left, asking if I'd look after the kid if anything happened to her. I just couldn't, man."

Becca felt sick to her stomach. Sicker than she had felt all week. She was staring at her father. A stranger she had been afraid of for years. A man who lurked around as she wandered through town. He had been keeping one hell of a secret for so long.

"Was she ... was she sick?" asked Becca. "Everybody tells me she had leukemia."

Paul shook his head slowly and sadly. "Nuh-uh. Healthy as a horse."

"Then what really happened?"

"She had you out in St. Aub and they dragged her back home right after. She was dead the next day."

"How?"

"They killed her."

"Who?"

The door crashed open. Travis and Mr. Valcourt charged in behind two RCMP officers. The four of them started yelling and barking orders at Paul and Becca. Becca stepped back. Travis rushed toward her, but she didn't want him — she wanted answers.

James lingered in the doorway. She tried calling out to him, but Travis caught her in a bearhug, squeezing the breath out of her.

"Jesus, Becca," he sighed. "You scared me."

"Travis—"

The officers clubbed Paul over the back of the head. He dropped to the floor. Becca cried out, twisting in Travis's strong arms to stop them. They continued to kick and punch and hold him down. Mr. Valcourt loomed over them with his arms crossed.

"Good work, men," he said, as they hoisted Paul to his feet and dragged him out. Mr. Valcourt turned to Becca. "I'm so sorry, my dear."

Sobbing, Becca fought to get past them and follow Paul, but they wouldn't let her go. "Please, I need—"

"I know." Mr. Valcourt bumped Travis aside and held Becca at arm's length. He touched her face, making her skin crawl. "You were so brave and I'm sorry that horrible person has tried to ruin your big day. He needs to be put down like a dog."

"I'll do it," offered Travis, and Becca wasn't sure if he was serious or not. "No one touches my girlfriend."

"I'm not your—" She stared at the doorway and caught a glimpse of James as he turned and walked away.

Chapter 18

ll Becca could think about as she stood on stage was the horrible beatdown the officers delivered to Paul. *My father?* They bashed his head in and dragged him away. They had probably thrown him in jail and god knows what they would do to him there. She felt awful.

No one had asked her what had happened; they all had assumed the worst.

She tried to explain to Travis, but he kept shushing her and holding her to his chest. "It's okay. It's over now. He won't ever hurt you again. I promise."

And then Mr. Valcourt rambled on and on about how inconvenient the timing of this was, and that he understood this had turned into a very unpleasant day, but that it would be best for everyone if she could pull herself together and make an appearance on stage.

"After all, that's why everyone's here," he said. "They came to see you."

"I don't think I can," said Becca, sniveling.

Mr. Valcourt's face hardened and he cocked his head to one side. "Oh, that would be a shame. And then imagine how much worse your day would get if you also got some bad news about your grandmother."

Wiping her nose with a tissue, Becca met his cold eyes. Travis may not have understood what his father was implying, but Becca read the subtext loud and clear. She bit down on her rage and glared at him. "Yeah," she agreed. "So I hope she won't mind if I go through with the coronation."

He smiled. "She won't. Now compose yourself and get cleaned up. I'll give you twenty minutes." He checked his watch. "No, make it fifteen." He snapped his fingers at Travis. "Help her, will you?"

Becca did her best to tidy up while Travis uselessly offered her paper towels. "You know, for makeup and stuff." By the time Mr. Valcourt returned to get the show on the road, Becca was as ready as she was going to be.

She stood in the wings with Travis, watching Mr. Valcourt stroll across the stage and approach the podium. Before he even grinned into the microphone, a hush settled over the crowd. He began to talk about Becca as if he knew her personally and what a fine girl she was and how she upholds everything beautiful about the honored role of Harvest Queen. He prattled on about what the title means and its importance in their town — but it was all vague and flowery language. He could have been describing a statue or a show pony. His speech gave no clues as to why it was so damn important.

Travis reached over and took her hand. "You look really beautiful today."

"Thanks," she muttered.

"I know you don't want to do this," he said. "So if you want, we can leave right now."

She stared at him in shock. *Was he serious?* "What about your dad?"

"He'll be pissed," Travis said, grinning. He looked like a very young version of his father. "But I believe you. You're the smartest person I know. If you think something's wrong here, then it's probably true."

"Thank you."

"I don't want us to fight anymore."

She squeezed his hand, tears stinging her eyes. "Travis…"

"Please join me in welcoming Miss Becca St. James!" boomed Mr. Valcourt.

A thunderous applause erupted in the auditorium. Becca's legs turned to jelly. She wanted to take Travis up on his offer. She wanted to get in his Firebird and drive far, far away. But she couldn't shake the haunting thought of what Mr. Valcourt might do to Gran.

She slipped her hand out of Travis's grip and forced a smile. "Thanks, but I have a job to do," she said.

He punched her gently on the shoulder and grinned.

"Just testing you. I knew you'd make the right decision."

Her heart sank. *It was a* test? *What a lowdown sneaky thing to do!* She forced a smile and replied, "It's my civic duty, Travis."

Becca walked across the stage. She began to sweat under the hot overhead lights. Wearing a jean jacket was a bad idea, but it was too late to change.

She joined Mr. Valcourt at the podium. He patted her shoulder. *Good girl.* Then he lifted the mike from its stand, walking all around the stage as he spoke about their shared love for the town. The audience clapped.

He waved over Travis, who strutted out, blowing kisses into the crowd. Travis positioned himself behind Becca and picked up the tiara. She craned her neck to see what he was doing. He hissed at her to face the front. Her smile tightened as she forced herself to look ahead.

The audience was filled with neighbors and people she knew from around town. Candace, Erin and their lunk-head boyfriends had moved up to the front row. Cyndy the hairdresser was there, as was Mr. Handy. Sadie had parked her wheelchair in the middle aisle, her gaggle of exercise gals seated nearby.

Becca searched for James and Mrs. Martin, but they were too far back.

As her gaze drifted over the sea of people, one thing was clear. No one smiled. They glared at her. Jaws were set on edge and shoulders were hunched up defensively. People she knew and had been friendly with looked like they wanted to tear her apart.

Is that what happened to my mom? she wondered.

Then she blinked and everyone looked normal again.

Travis set the tiara on her head. Though it appeared delicate on the pillow, it weighed heavily and dug into her scalp. She startled when he touched her with it, but she laughed it off as if she was just so happy and excited to be there, and not terrified about what may come next.

Mr. Valcourt began to sing. Becca's eyes widened. *Oh, god, please no.*

He had a big, deep voice, and the song sounded like a medley of three other pop songs with new lyrics added. He glided across the stage, holding his arm so everyone would stare at Becca. All she wanted in that moment was for a trap door to magically open under her feet. If that was how the other queens died, then it would be a goddamn blessing.

When the song ended, Mr. Valcourt led the audience in a round of applause. He stepped beside her, gripping her arm with his free hand, and stuck the microphone in her face. "And how do you feel this afternoon, Miss Becca?"

"Just fine, thank you."

"Have you picked out your dress for the big event next Saturday?"

"No, sir. Not yet."

He shared a look of brow-raising surprise with the audience. *"Not yet?* You have a week, girl! We're going to have to make sure you get on it."

She smiled, like this was all a dream come true. Like

her Gran wasn't in the hospital or that she hadn't just met her father in the utilities room. She smiled like she was living the perfect life. To do otherwise would mean bad things. "Yes, sir. I'm looking forward to it."

* * *

As the hall cleared out, Becca sneaked out the back door. She hoped to avoid everyone but James. She needed to talk to him.

But someone else slipped out the back door too, and she knew her day wasn't over yet.

Mr. Valcourt walked down the steps until his shiny dress shoes touched the gravel lot. He made a face at the grit and dust that accumulated on the hem of his pants, as he turned to speak to her. "You did a good job in there," he said. "I take it you're coming around to the idea."

"Yes, sir," she said.

Mr. Valcourt could read subtext too. "The Harvest Festival is very important to this town. I'd hate to see some sniveling, ungrateful teenager throw away an incredible opportunity like this."

"Me too."

He put his hands on his hips. "What did Paul Leblanc say to you?"

"Nothing."

"You were in there for quite a while."

Becca's face burned, and she wouldn't have been surprised if she stayed red after the day was done. She had oscillated between scared and angry and embarrassed all afternoon, and each emotion made her skin flush. "He was scaring me. I told him to let me out. We went back and forth like that for a while."

"Travis says he heard talking."

"Travis *wasn't in there*, was he?"

"No, and I don't know what sort of high school games you're playing with him and this other boy, James-something, but I think you need to start acting like a proper lady and not some cheap—" He caught himself when Becca's jaw dropped. He straightened his tie. "Never mind. It's none of my business."

That's right, she thought, holding her tongue.

"I just want to know what Paul said so I know what to tell the police."

"Shouldn't *I* tell them? He came after me, not you."

"True, but I think you're a little disturbed after that interaction. It must have been frightening to be trapped in that room with such an unstable person. You're already under so much stress as it is. The police will understand if I provide a statement on your behalf."

The cold look in his eye told her that he was going to do it anyway. Becca needed to get to the RCMP station as soon as possible. Maybe her own words would clear Paul's name and get him out of there.

First, she needed to make Mr. Valcourt go away. "Okay, whatever. Can I go home now?"

"Of course." He stepped aside.

Starting off in the direction of home, she glanced back

at the community hall. Mr. Valcourt stood where she left him, watching her. When she was far enough away to disappear around a couple of parked cars, she stepped onto the sidewalk toward the RCMP station.

* * *

James caught up to Becca a few blocks later. He crossed her path and she jumped back with a yelp. "It's okay, it's just me," he said, holding his hands out.

She put a hand to her chest and closed her eyes. "Oh, my god. You scared me."

"I'm sorry. Helluva day you've had."

"Tell me about it," she said. "I have to get to the police station right now."

"Where is it?"

"Two more blocks. I have to talk to Paul Leblanc."

"I figured. He was in the same yearbook as your mom. That's what you wanted me to find, right? I think they must've been a couple."

"Why didn't you tell me? You said you were going to look into it."

"I know, I just—" *Travis messed with my head.* "I'm sorry. It's been a crazy week."

"I know." She kept walking, faster this time. He matched her pace so they could go together.

James didn't want to tell her that he actually believed her ex-boyfriend when he said had they slept together and then went down a jealousy spiral that made him not want to help her, even though who she slept with was none of his damned business. Instead he said, "I'm sorry."

"That's okay," she said. "I like your new glasses, by the way."

"Oh, yeah, thanks." He stole a glance at her. Her cheeks were pink, but it was probably from walking at such a fast pace, and not from any kind of feelings for him. He decided that was fine. They would just be friends and he would help her as he would any friend.

The RCMP station was a small brick structure with few windows and a secure entrance. No one could walk in without being assessed by the desk officer and then buzzed in.

But James and Becca didn't need to be buzzed in. The door swung open as two EMTs carried out a black body bag on a stretcher. James had a bad feeling. He grabbed Becca's arm, holding her back from going any closer. She pulled, but he was stronger.

"Becca, don't…"

An RCMP officer followed the EMTs to the waiting ambulance. They loaded the body in and slammed the doors as Becca began firing off questions.

"Who is that? What happened?"

The officer, one of the men who had dragged Paul Leblanc out of the community hall only a few hours ago, scratched his bald head. "Nothing to see here, kids. Better go on home."

Becca trembled. "Please — tell me."

"I don't know what to tell you," the officer said, which

was what guilty people liked to say when they had to break bad news. "Life on the street took a toll on the guy, I guess."

"No…"

James steered her away from the flashing ambulance lights and the disinterested officer. "It's okay," he said.

She sniffled, looking over her shoulder. "I think he knew what happened. He was the missing piece. And now…"

James followed her gaze. Across the parking lot, Declan Valcourt climbed into his LeBaron and drove away.

Chapter 19

Morganville was abuzz on Sunday. The carnival equipment company had come into town early that morning to set up on the high school grounds. It was the largest piece of land in the most central part of town that would serve the most people. Tents were raised and rides were constructed.

Declan Valcourt and the town council members took a tour to see all the work being done, while a reporter from the *Morganville News* trailed them to take their photos. They stopped and smiled and pointed at random half-built rides. Mr. Valcourt dropped a few sound bites and everyone laughed and clapped each other on the back.

It was a beautiful day.

Across town, James met Becca at their usual spot in the library. She had sneaked in a travel mug of instant coffee. Dark circles had formed under her eyes and she wore her hair in a messy ponytail.

"You don't look like you slept well," he noted.

"How can I sleep with less than a week to live?" she grumbled. "I'll sleep when I'm dead."

"Becca…" He didn't like hearing her talk like that, not while she was still alive and kicking. Not when there was still a chance to do something.

She paused, staring over his shoulder.

He followed her gaze to a display of newspapers. Notable front pages from the past two decades of the *Morganville News* had been framed and hung on the wall.

"We can't do this alone," she said. "We're just kids."

"So what? There must be something we can do to shut this down."

"There is." She smiled. It was the first real smile he had seen on her face in days. "Think you can type up all your notes while I make a few photocopies?"

"Yeah, sure," he said, flipping through his notebook. "What're you thinking?"

Two hours later, they banged on the door of the *Morganville News* office, not far from the library on main street. While its front door was open to the public Monday to Friday, no one manned the front desk on the weekend, nor was anyone required to be in the office.

But Becca and James had to see if someone was there.

They didn't have a lot of time, and though sliding a package of all their notes and archival information through the mail slot was an option, they couldn't risk it getting lost in the mail.

Luckily for them, reporter Phil Michaels was hanging around. He preferred to spend his Sunday afternoons writing his columns so he could slack off and wander around town talking to people during the week.

He peered through the glass window before he opened the door to the two shiny-faced teenagers waiting eagerly outside. "Hello…?"

"Hello, sir," said Becca. "Are you a reporter?"

"I dabble," he said, because Phil was proud of his dry sense of humor and his noncommittal answers. Being the smartest and vaguest guy in the room had always been one of his life's goals. But then he figured they were just kids and probably intellectually inferior. He stuck out a hand. "Phil Michaels. What can I do ya for?"

"I'm James and this is Becca."

"We need your help," Becca said.

"We learned something terrible about the Harvest Festival and we hope you'll print it in tomorrow's paper," said James, opening the package of everything they had collected and offered Phil a folder.

"Every Harvest Queen for the past 70 years has been killed," she added.

Phil's bushy brows raised, and he took the folder. He held back from saying "neat-o" because having a mildly morbid fascination with the dark side of humanity was something he could share only with other inkslingers.

He thumbed through their notes. It was all neatly packaged and easy to read. "We oughta offer you two internships," he said. "You've done a better job here than any of our last student reporters."

"We're not looking for jobs, sir," said Becca. "We just want someone to stop the festival."

"I don't think I can do that," said Phil. "I just write stories."

"We know," said James. "And we've done everything we can—"

"And we've tried talking to the reeve, but no one wants to really look at this information."

He squinted, rubbing his round chin. "You're not pulling my leg, are you? This isn't some kind of prank?"

They shook their heads, staring at him with wide, saucer eyes. Phil always patted himself on the back for being a great judge of character. He could suss out when a source lied to him or when they were holding back. These two kids were willing to lay everything on the table, and it was starting to spook him.

He would have to look into it himself, but maybe there was something to their little theory.

"All the queens were killed, you say?"

"We don't know the exact cause of death, but definitely dead right after the opening night of the festival," said Becca.

"Huh." He gave her a closer look. "You're the one they selected for this year. St. John?"

"St. James," she corrected. "You'll see in the file that my mom was one of the past queens."

"Uh-huh…" He skimmed through until he found the

list of names. "If this is true, you must be real nervous."

She nodded.

"Why don't you quit?" he asked.

"I tried," she said. "People keep telling me it's my 'civic duty.'"

"That sounds ominous." He took one more look through the folder. "Alright, how about this: The Monday news has already gone to print, but I can pitch this to my editor tomorrow and we'll see what comes of it."

Becca and James exchanged an anxious look that said they didn't think Phil was going to move the story up the chain of command.

"Look, it's the best I can do," he said. "My editor likes to spend these last few nice weekends up at the lake. There's no way I'll be able to reach him. But consider it a blessing because it'll give me time to work on my own pitch and do a little digging. Okay?"

Becca reluctantly agreed. She ripped a piece of paper out of her notebook and scribbled down her name and phone number. "Will you please call me, good or bad news? I just want to know what happens next."

He glanced at the number and folded the paper into quarters before stuffing it into his shirt pocket. "You got it, kid. Now go on. Enjoy the rest of your weekend."

* * *

Becca did not enjoy the rest of her weekend. James took her to get something to eat. He was worried that without her grandmother around to fix up meals, Becca was going to waste away. She kept telling him she could take care of herself, but she also didn't fight it when he took her to the burger place for a double cheeseburger, fries, and a vanilla shake.

The shake made Becca's stomach ache, and by the time she got home, all she wanted to do was go to bed.

She couldn't fall asleep or get comfortable, thanks to her too-full stomach and nausea about everything, but at some point after the sun had set, she fell asleep only to be woken up the next morning by the telephone's shrill ring.

She tried to hide under her pillow. It was probably someone calling to bother her about Harvest Queen stuff. Erin and Candace couldn't stop talking about what kind of dress she was going to wear, even though she didn't give a shit. The town could parade her around in a burlap sack for all she cared. It just didn't matter.

It matters to the town. She imagined their cruelly twisted faces staring at her on the stage.

She still had to get to the bottom of it, and when the ringing stopped only to start up again after a pause, she realized it could be Phil Michaels calling with an update.

She jumped out of bed and ran downstairs. "Hello?" she breathed into the phone. "Mr. Michaels?"

"No," said a clinical female voice. "This is Nurse Tina at St. Aubergine General. I'm sorry to inform you that your grandmother's condition worsened and she is no longer with us."

"What?" Becca croaked.

Nurse Tina relayed the same message again as Becca sank down to the floor, clutching the phone. She wished she had misheard the nurse.

"No…"

"I'm so sorry, dear."

"What happened?"

Something brushed against the phone on the other end of the call, as if the phone was changing hands. Becca didn't notice it right away because blood was pounding in her ears and she was trying so hard not to lose it, not yet. She had to be strong for Gran and figure out what to do next.

Mr. Valcourt's voice oozed through the phone. "Hello, Becca. I see I caught you before school."

Her blood ran ice cold. *What is he doing there?* She had a bad feeling. "What do you want?"

"I wanted to tell you that I was with your grandmother in her final moments. She didn't die alone."

Becca covered her mouth to hold in a sob. Tears streamed down her face. *I wasn't there. I should've been there. This is all my fault. All my fault!*

"It's too bad," he said. "Perhaps if you hadn't been chasing down reporters, you could have been at the hospital with her. What a terrible shame. I know something like that would follow me to the grave."

Shoulders shaking, Becca wiped her eyes. The tears wouldn't stop. "You—" She choked on her words.

"Watch what you say next," he warned. The tone of his voice hit her like a whip. "There are still a few more days until the festival. I suggest you get your act together. No more running around spreading rumors. Understood?"

She croaked out an affirmative response.

"Good girl," he said. "Now, you have a busy week ahead, so I'll have my assistant take care of Dottie's funeral arrangements." He rattled off a few other administrative tasks that he was also responsible for and then ended the call.

Becca, meanwhile, released the phone. It sprang up on its cord like a bungee jumper, then dangled over her head as she curled into a ball and sobbed on the floor.

Chapter 20

*O*n Monday, Becca wasn't at school. On Tuesday, after spending all morning trying to find her, James overheard her bitchy girlfriends say something about her grandmother passing away. *That's why she's not here.*

Despite that awful news, he needed to talk to her about the Tuesday paper. There was nothing in the day's edition about anything they handed over to the reporter, and he was starting to get antsy.

By two o'clock, he couldn't take it anymore and faked a stomachache. His English teacher, Mr. Williams, sent him to the nurse's office, but James took a detour out the front door and ran across campus. Once he was far enough from the school grounds, he slowed his pace and hoofed it to the *Morganville News* office.

The newsroom was abuzz with staff and the woman at the front desk politely asked if he had an appointment. James could see Phil Michaels across the bullpen and pointed him out, stabbing a finger at him.

"Mr. Michaels!" he called.

The newsroom grew quiet as the other reporters and editors stopped to see what was going on. Phil adjusted his tie, well aware of everyone's eyes on him. He pushed out of his creaky office chair and went to greet James.

"Hey, kid," he said. "This isn't the best time."

James wiped sweat off his brow. "Becca has four days left, *five tops.* What's taking so long?"

"It's complicated, uh— what was your name again?"

"James Martin."

"Well, James Martin, it's complicated. You wouldn't understand."

"Try me."

Scratching his chin, Phil looked the kid over; he secreted desperation. Phil hooked an arm around the kid's neck and steered him toward the door. In a loud voice, he said, "That's enough. No more pranks around here. Time to go home." As James started to protest, Phil jabbed him in the ribs and in a near-whisper, said, "Meet me in the alley in five. And keep quiet."

Too stunned to question him, James did as he was told.

The alley behind the *Morganville News* office was shared by a Chinese food restaurant and an auto body shop. It smelled of food grease and motor oil. A pile of cigarette butts had accumulated by the rear door of the newspaper. James leaned on a drum of grease and waited five minutes, then ten. It was almost twenty minutes later when Phil sneaked out with a pack of cigarettes and a lighter.

Fuming, James marched up to him. "What took you so long?"

"Calm down," he grumbled, lighting a cigarette. "And keep your voice down. I don't have a lot of time here."

"I almost left."

"You should have. Leave this whole stinking town if you've got the balls, kid."

"What did you find out?"

"I checked your research. It's good work. You should consider a career in journalism — you know, if you like being underpaid and overworked," he snickered. James sighed, crossing his arms. "Alright, relax. I'll tell ya — you're right. Something's rotten with this festival business, and like I just said, if you and your girlfriend can get outta town, you'd better do it soon. Someone's been killing these girls as part of the festivities."

"Like a ritual?"

Phil held up his hands. "Hey, I don't know anything about rituals. All I know is that a lot of the old-timers and councilmen think having this festival brings prosperity to the town and to them. And all it costs is a girl's life every couple of decades."

A human sacrifice. James ran a hand through his hair. He couldn't believe this, but also it made so much sense. "But you're not going to print the story?"

"Wish I could, but I can't. Declan Valcourt and his council cronies had their lawyer send a cease-and-desist to my editor yesterday. You know what that means?"

"Yeah, I think so."

"It means if I write this story, they'll sic a big, fat lawsuit on my ass."

James dropped his hands to his side. "So what do we do?"

Phil took a drag on his cigarette, squinting up at the sun. "I don't know, kid. You could try to get outta town, but it looks like that didn't work for Bethany St. James. I heard they dragged that poor girl back kicking and screaming right after her kid was born."

James's heart ached at the thought.

"Or you could stick around and see what happens. Maybe things won't be as bad this time around."

James felt a tension headache coming on. He muttered goodbye as he turned to leave.

"Just be careful," added Phil. The door to the office opened. A couple of reporters stuck their heads out, watching Phil. They called him over. Phil gave them a half-hearted wave before stamping out his cigarette. "This thing goes deep."

* * *

Deep. James couldn't fathom how deep until he got home and saw his mother sitting at the breakfast bar staring at a stack of bills. Her eyes were puffy and rimmed red, and she had been chain smoking.

The door slammed shut behind him and Mrs. Martin gasped. She scrambled to push all the bills under a file folder as James approached. "Oh, hi, dear. I didn't hear you come in."

"What's that?"

"Nothing. Not important."

"Looks important."

"Well, it's nothing you need to worry about."

James spied the bright red PAST DUE stamp on one of the envelopes. "Mom..."

"It's nothing!" she snapped.

He shook his head and stormed off to his room. He didn't slam the door — every teenager's way of saying *fuck you*. She was already hurting. So he sat on his bed and picked up a book he had to read for English. He couldn't focus because he kept wondering why his mother hadn't bothered to ask why he was home so early.

Around dinner time, she shuffled down the hall and poked her head in. The sky outside had darkened. The change in light had been so gradual that James didn't realize he was squinting to see the words in his book.

"James," she said, a waver in her voice. She clutched the folded stack of bills. "I'm sorry."

Putting the book aside, he sat up and turned on his lamp. "What's wrong?"

She took a seat at the foot of his bed. "I tried *really hard.*" She laid out the bills on her lap. "I thought I could make a go of it here, but nothing's working."

Trying to keep a brave face, she explained everything. She had already been behind in paying their bills when they moved to Morganville, but at the time, she at least had some contacts and existing clients to work with. She even made some connections that were throwing work her way. But then in the last week, each and every client called to put an end to their business contract. Work dried up and she saw her income stream turn to dust.

"I don't know what to do."

She broke down and sobbed into her hands. James put his arms around her and hugged her as tightly as he could. He didn't know what else to do either.

* * *

Friday. Becca laid in bed, staring at the ceiling. Her tears had dried up (for the moment). She laced her fingers across her stomach and imagined pushing herself downward until she broke through her bed, through the floor, through the house, and disappeared into a deep, dark hole.

The only thing that got her out of bed was the phone ringing. After trying to ignore it one night, she ended up getting a visit from Mr. Valcourt. He wandered through Gran's living room, picking up dusty trinkets and placing them back down, slightly off from where they had originally been. He moved into the kitchen and made her a sandwich and a glass of Tang.

She didn't want him in her house and the sandwich was

dry, sticking in her throat. She forced it down and responded to his small talk. Then he reached across the table and grabbed her hand. He clenched it until she feared her bones would break.

"You're going to listen and listen good," he said. "When that goddamn phone rings, you get your lazy ass downstairs and answer it. None of this moping around bullshit."

Tears filled her eyes. "Please," she said. "I can't do this. Not now. I need some time. My Gran—"

"I know what happened to Dottie. You don't need to remind me."

"Just a couple of weeks? After the funeral?"

"No, the date stands. You're the Harvest Queen on Saturday night. No excuses."

He left her alone after that. His assistant called once to arrange a hair appointment on Saturday and to ask about her favorite color, but after that she didn't hear from anyone. Not even James.

On Friday afternoon, Erin and Candace arrived with her dress. Since Becca was too bereft to go shopping, Mr. Valcourt allowed the two girls and his assistant to sort out the fashion arrangements. Becca answered the door, surprised that they were delivering a dress and not sitting in class.

"Didn't you hear?" said Erin, smacking her gum. "We're on the dress committee."

"You wouldn't pick one, so we did it for you," said Candace.

"I think we did a perfect job," said Erin.

They unveiled the dress in the living room. Erin held it up — a beautiful off-white gown. Form-fitting around the bust and then flowing from the waist down.

"You'll look like a bride, but like, not," Erin said.

When she slumped on the couch and tried to talk about her grandmother, the two girls shifted uncomfortably. Candace at least patted her back and said, "Try to feel better."

Becca began to cry and they left in a hurry. Then she dragged herself back to her room, tossed the dress on her desk and laid in bed, staring at the ceiling for hours.

When there was nothing left to do, she sat up and wiped her face. Her eyes felt dry from so much weeping. She got dressed, went downstairs, and called James.

As usual, his mother answered. "So nice to hear from you, Becca," she said. It sounded like Mrs. Martin had been doing some crying of her own.

"Same," she said. "Is James there?"

"Yes, just a sec."

As Becca waited, she chewed on her fingernails. She hadn't indulged in this bad habit since junior high when Gran tried everything to help her stop. Something had worked and ever since, Becca had beautiful, long nails. But tonight she needed some control over her body. She needed to feel empowered. A few ragged nails were a good start.

"Hey," said James. "Everything okay?"

"No," she said. "Feel like going for a drive?"

Chapter 21

When Becca climbed into the passenger seat of his mom's station wagon, James asked, "So where are we going?"

She was bundled up in a coat with the fur-lined collar flipped up around her face. "Anywhere."

James didn't ask for further directions. He just put the car in drive and hit the gas. He cruised through the neighborhood and past the elementary school while she stared out the window. Neither said anything until they neared the church.

"I don't know what else to do," she said.

"Me neither," he said, adjusting his glasses. "Maybe it'll be okay? Maybe we're blowing this out of proportion?"

"No," she said.

"Yeah," he agreed. "I don't think so either."

"I just wish I knew what's going to happen," she said bitterly.

James thought for a minute. *Should I tell her?* He had to. He figured he would want to know if he was in the same position. "I talked to that reporter the other day, after he didn't run our story."

"Oh, yeah?" She rubbed her brow.

"It sounds like the Harvest Festival has something to do with, um, human sacrifice."

"Shit," she said.

"Sorry."

"No, it's alright… I mean, it's *not* alright. It's just…" She didn't bother to finish her sentence. What was the point?

James couldn't take it anymore. He hit the gas and started toward the western road out of town. He would take Becca into the city. Hide her at a friends' house. Drop her off at a shelter if necessary. Whatever it took. He wasn't going to let her die.

"What're you doing?" she asked, sitting up straighter.

"We're leaving," he said.

"What about your mom? What about—?" She twisted around in her seatbelt to look at him.

He grimaced, his face lit up by the dashboard. "Doesn't matter. Fuck everybody."

Silence filled the car. Becca reached across the seat and took his hand. She unbuckled and scooted over to be closer to him. When she spoke again, her voice was soft and low. "You don't have to stick your neck out for me. You might get into trouble."

He squeezed her hand right back, rubbing his thumb over her knuckles. "We're in this together."

The road ahead, just before the underpass out of town was blocked by pylons and crowd-control barriers. RCMP officers redirected traffic and waved in vehicles entering the town. No one was leaving, at least not from this end.

Becca and James leaned forward. "There's probably an accident up ahead, that's all," he said.

As they neared the roadblock, he rolled down the window. "Is there a problem, officer?"

The cop peered inside and studied Becca, who shrank back down inside her coat. "Good evening, Miss St. James. Out for a drive?"

She nodded.

"Good night for it," he said. "Road ahead is blocked off for tomorrow's festival. Wouldn't want anything to happen to you on the highway tonight." With a tip of his cap, he backed off and directed them to turn around.

James wasn't deterred. He spun the car around and headed for the other end of town. His stomach flip-flopped as red-and-blue flashing lights appeared in the distance. Another damn police barricade cut them off.

"Shit." He pounded the steering wheel.

"Now what?" she asked.

"There's only one other way out," he said. "It's going to be blocked too."

"For me, yeah, but maybe not for you." She climbed

into the backseat, tore off her coat, and wedged herself under the bench. "Gimme your jacket."

He took off his jacket and turned up the heat in the car. He doubted her plan would work; the cops weren't letting anyone leave town. But they had to try.

He drove toward the last exit. This road turned into a secondary highway that would take them past a few pig farms. There usually wasn't a lot of traffic unless you lived on one of the acreages or wanted to take the long route to Fort Saskin, a town only slightly larger than Morganville.

There was no barricade — just a black Pontiac parked haphazardly across the two lanes and four young men standing guard. Travis Valcourt leaned against the driver's side door with his arms crossed and that goddamn smirk on his face.

James slowed down.

"What?" asked Becca, muffled under the seat.

"Travis," he whispered, trying not to move his lips. "Shit."

He considered making a sharp maneuver around them, but his mom's station wagon was clunky, and the steering was lousy. If anything, he would likely veer into the ditch and end up rolling the car.

Travis curled his finger — *come here* — as James rolled to a stop. He grinned. When he was alongside the car, he rapped his knuckles on the glass. James cracked the window and decided to go on the offensive.

"Get outta the road," he said. "You're gonna get hit."

"Don't think so, chump. We're volunteer RCMP officers tonight, making sure everyone sticks around for the festival tomorrow."

"I'll be back," said James. "I just have to pick up some milk."

"Oh, yeah? What's wrong with the milk at the IGA?"

James swallowed. "They're all out."

"Shame. Guess you're gonna have to do without."

One of Travis's friends — Heath or Mark, James wasn't sure which — sidled up to the other side of the car. He pressed his dumb country boy face against the glass, leaving a smear of grease where his forehead had been. "Hey, Trav." He waved Travis over, but Travis didn't budge. "Come look at this."

Shit. James tightened his grip on the wheel. He thought about gunning through their check-stop and tearing down the highway like a bat out of hell.

"I know," said Travis. "Pretty sure he's got Becca back there."

James's blood went cold. *How could they...?* He peered over his shoulder. While Becca's plan had been clever, she wasn't able to hide completely; her long hair splayed across the floorboard.

Becca sat up. The jig was up. She rolled down her window. "This is serious, Travis. You have to let us leave. Please."

He stuck out his chin. "Ahh, I *love* when you beg. Just like that night when you wanted me to fuck you."

"Travis," she warned. There was an edge to her voice.

"I get it," he said. "This loser probably can't even get it up for you."

"Fuck off, man," James snapped. "Just let us go."

Travis backed away from the car with his hands up. "Easy there, gang. Now I could let you go, but..." He reached around and pulled a police radio from his back pocket. "I'd have to call it in. And I wouldn't be very nice about it."

"I thought you cared about me," said Becca. "You wanted me to say I love you?"

He chuckled, glancing back at his boys. "That's just something I like to hear girls say when I'm banging them."

"You're an asshole."

"And you know I can't let some other guy ride off into the sunset with you. It wouldn't be good for my image."

"Then why don't *you* take her?" James offered. He hated himself for the suggestion, but if it was the only way to save Becca's life, he had to do it. "Just get her as far away from here as you can."

Travis raised an eyebrow.

"Don't stop driving," James continued. "I'll go straight home. I won't say a thing to anybody."

"James," Becca said softly, though they both stared at Travis. This was his chance to be the big hero.

Travis's gaze dropped to the ground and he backed away from the station wagon. "My dad..."

Coward, James thought, but didn't say it. *You have a chance to save your girlfriend. No one would stop you,*

you son of a bitch. You fucking coward.

Becca squeezed James's shoulder as she leaned forward. "Drive."

He lifted his foot off the brake and made a U-turn, taking them away from Travis and his friends. The farm boy grunted something about why they were letting them go, but all Travis did was scowl.

* * *

"You were going to hand me over to Travis just like that?" Becca asked when they were back to cruising up and down main street.

"If it got you away from this place, then yeah."

She settled in the backseat and held herself. "I don't want to go anywhere with him. Travis is a creep."

"Then why were you with him?"

"I don't know." She shrugged. "I guess it was exciting when he noticed me. We'd been in school together for a long time, running in different circles." Her friends had moved away around the time they started junior high, so she was on her own most of the time. "He just started talking to me one day and I thought it was a mistake — like he must've thought I was some other girl. But then he just kept coming around and my Gran seemed to really like him…"

"Do you think your Gran would've liked me?"

He watched her in the rearview mirror and caught the corner of her mouth lift. The evening had been filled with sadness and defeat, but at least he made her smile. He decided not to press her on the question and kept driving.

Then her hand settled on his shoulder and gave him another squeeze. He felt firm and strong under his thin, pale t-shirt. "Pull over somewhere," she said.

He turned onto a quiet street where there were a few scattered houses barely standing. Across the road was a narrow parking lot overrun with grass and weeds. James parked behind a tall, rickety fence that blocked the homeowners' view of the overgrown lot. It was so dark and quiet that when he rolled the window down for some air, they heard small creatures croaking and chirping all around.

Becca's hand moved down from his shoulder and over his chest. Her breath was hot on his neck. He stared straight ahead, hoping she couldn't feel his thundering heart.

"I don't think I'll ever be able to thank you for trying to help me," she whispered.

"I didn't do anything. I couldn't even get you some- where safe." He gripped the wheel, shaking his head. *"This is bullshit."*

"James."

"No, I'm sorry. I can't—" He twisted around. "This isn't fair. You don't deserve this." He took off his glasses and started polishing one of the lenses. "Let's ditch the car. Maybe we can sneak out on foot and—"

She turned his face to the side and kissed him. He stopped wiping his glasses and melted into her lips. When they parted, he stared at her, noticing she had begun to unbutton her blouse.

He ran his hand through her hair, stroking the side of her face, and pulled her back in for another yearning kiss. She leaned back, pulling him with her, and broke away only to say, "Come back here."

Hands shaking, he clicked off his seatbelt. His shoe caught on the gear shift as he climbed over the seat, and he frantically kicked it off only to bump his head on the domelight. When he finally made it over, he collapsed on top of her as she giggled.

"What's so funny?" he asked, sheepishly.

"Nothing. I just like you."

"I like you too."

She put her arms around him, pulling him down on top of her. She lifted a leg up and around his waist as he kissed her from her mouth, down her neck, and to her open shirt.

His heart pounded when she reached behind to unclasp her bra. The flimsy lace contraption slipped off her shoulders. He groaned, taking her in.

"You're beautiful," he murmured.

"James..." she whispered in his ear. "I don't want to die without having sex."

He froze. "But I thought Travis said—?"

"No. Whatever he said — *no.*"

"Oh."

Her hands went down to his belt buckle and tugged. "Please?" she asked, looking up at him.

His pants couldn't get any tighter at that moment, so

he felt relieved when she unbuckled and unzipped him. She reached in and grabbed him. He gasped, and when she started stroking him, he thought he was going to lose his mind.

"Have you ever...?"

"No," he said. "I mean, I had a girlfriend, and we did stuff, but — *oh, god...* "

She wriggled underneath him. He could feel the warmth of her skin and realized she had taken off her pants and underwear. He froze when she wrapped her legs around him. "It's okay," she said, guiding him. "I want you to."

"Are you sure?"

"Yes."

She held on as he pushed into her. The pressure was almost too much to bear, and she bit down on her lip. He paused to ask if she was okay. She nodded, encouraging him to keep going. They kissed, and a tear escaped from the corner of her eye.

Chapter 22

*S*taring at the wilted flowers, Becca knelt in her Gran's backyard garden. She wasn't allowed to go anywhere without supervision, but thank god Mr. Valcourt, his assistant, Travis, Candace and Erin, and hairstylist Cyndy didn't give a shit that she wanted to wander around in the yard. Candace warned her about getting grass stains on her dress, but when Becca ignored her and went out the door, everybody just shrugged.

She was the queen after all, and her wish was their command.

Unfortunately, her only real wish — other than not dying or canceling the festival — was to remain in James's arms and for last night to never end.

Curled up in the back of the station wagon, they made

love and talked into the early morning hours. He offered to hide her at his house, but they both knew that would only delay the inevitable.

"There has to be *something* we can do," he said.

"There's not."

So she returned home to sleep in her own bed, basking in the afterglow of slow, sweet, clumsy sex with a boy she was falling for. By late afternoon, Mr. Valcourt and the others descended upon the house, banging on the door and tearing her out of a beautiful dream.

Becca didn't fight it, but she didn't help either, forcing Erin and Candace to dress her. The two girls complained the entire time. *Well, if they want their queen so badly, they're going to work for it.*

"What if..." James had asked in the back of the station wagon, their naked bodies entangled. "What if they want you for a *virgin* sacrifice?"

"Virginity is a construct — it doesn't actually exist," she replied.

"Doesn't mean Valcourt and the council or the rest of the town doesn't believe in it. What then?"

"Then consider this my final act of defiance," she replied, climbing on top of him.

Becca smiled, relishing the moment, as Erin zipped up the back of her dress.

After Cyndy styled her hair, they had an hour to kill before it was time. Time for what, Becca still didn't know.

While everyone waited around, Becca was allowed to wander. When no one was looking, she slipped out of her ridiculously high heels and tossed them behind a bush, exchanging them for her white sneakers. They were still a bit stained from the first day of school, but at least she could move better in them.

"What can I do?" James had asked when he dropped her off. "I can't just leave you."

Her chin trembled as she tried not to think about how this was her last kiss. "Learn everything you can," she said. "Get this story out there. Don't let them get away with this."

She knew that wasn't what he wanted to hear, but they were all out of ideas. As he hugged her before saying their final goodbyes, she felt his tears on her shoulder.

Mr. Valcourt's assistant, Lois, snapped her fingers from the patio, waking Becca from the bittersweet memory. She glanced over her shoulder at the woman, and Candace and Erin, their arms crossed and a concerned look on their faces.

How closely were they watching me?

"It's time to go." Lois pointed to the tiny watch on her wrist as if Becca could see the time from that far away. "Let's move. No more moping about."

Becca clawed one more thing from Gran's garden and tucked it in her sneaker before standing up and brushing herself off. A bit of dirt smeared on her dress. *Good*, she thought bitterly.

When she rejoined the group on the patio, Candace and Erin fussed with her dress, complaining about the dirt. *Don't look too closely.* Candace reached down to fluff up the bottom of the dress, and for a moment Becca's ankles and sneakers were exposed. Anyone looking at her feet might have seen the small gray handle sticking out of her shoe.

Becca swatted them away. "It's fine. Let's go."

They gathered on the front lawn as a black stretch limousine parked in front of the house. Lois insisted everyone take photos with it. With her handbag hanging from the crook of her elbow, she waved everybody into frame and snapped several pictures with her huge camera. Becca made sure to blink at every moment.

Another act of defiance.

Then Travis, in a suit and tie just like his dear old dad, offered her his arm. She scoffed at him. "I don't need a date."

Scowling, Travis said, "I told you, Dad. She's being a real—"

Mr. Valcourt held up his hand. "I know what she's being, son." He stepped between them and lowered himself down to her level. "This is a very important day. I expect you to behave."

"Or what?" she shot back. "I'm all out of grandparents for you to murder."

He drew a sharp, whistling breath through his nostrils and took a step back. "Fine." He looked at Travis. "Sorry, son. You're going to have to take your own car. I'll make sure Becca gets where she needs to be."

"But, Dad…" Before Travis could complain, Mr. Valcourt opened the limo door and ushered Becca inside.

* * *

"It's a shame you and Travis couldn't work things out," said Mr. Valcourt, sitting across from Becca in the back of the limo. "He's a good kid, but doesn't always get a fair shake."

"Life isn't fair," Becca muttered. As the limo drove away, she watched her home disappear from view.

Mr. Valcourt opened a small compartment and took out two glasses and a bottle of some brown liquid. He poured two drinks and thrust one into her hands. The liquid sloshed on her dress, and she gave him a dirty look.

He threw back his drink with a shrug. "Who cares? No one's gonna see."

"I thought I'm supposed to go to the festival?"

"No," he said, pouring another drink. "The festival's for the town. Not you."

Becca felt mildly relieved. All night, she had thought about James's theory about human sacrifice. She imagined laying on an ancient altar with the whole town gathered around her. She was wearing a virginal white gown as Mr. Valcourt stood over her, brandishing an ornate dagger.

She found some comfort in picturing such an outcome. Though it would hurt to get stabbed in the gut and bleed out, she would at least know what to expect.

"So where am I going?"

Mr. Valcourt polished off another drink; poured himself another. He was getting drunk. His words began to slur together. He pointed at her own drink, still full to the brim. "Drink up. It'll take the edge off."

Becca was certain she wanted all her edges. "Where are you taking me?"

"Does it matter? It'll all be over soon."

"It matters to me," said Becca, voice wavering. "I'm here, aren't I? I'm committed to whatever the hell this is. I deserve to know."

He took another drink, slower this time. His bloodshot eyes drifted over her. "I'm not a bad guy."

I disagree.

"You ever learn about the trolley problem?" he asked.

"I don't think so."

"I think about it a lot. Especially with this whole thing." He waved at her. "There's a trolley. It's going fast, tearing down the tracks. It's headed straight for a bunch of people. They're all tied up and left on the tracks, like in those old western movies. And then there's me, or you, and you're next to the lever. You're far away, so you can't move the people yourself, but you can maybe see them. The only thing you can do is pull the lever. If you pull it, you'll switch the trolley onto another track, but what do you know? There's *a person* on the second track! So at this point, you can either do nothing — and the people will get run over — or you can pull the lever, kill just one to save the rest. What do you do?"

The limo came to a stop in the rocky parking lot of the decommissioned grain elevator on the edge of town. It wasn't nearly as tall as the church, but the old, faded green structure stretched high into the sky, casting a long, black shadow on anyone who dared wander past it.

The grain elevator was near the train tracks — could that be the literal "trolley problem" he was hinting at?

Becca frowned. "It's just a stupid hypothetical situation. It's not real."

He laughed, leaning toward her. "But it *is* real! That's my problem. You die or the town dies!"

Dropping her glass to the floor, she pressed herself against the seat to get as far away from him as she could. Her eyes darted around, searching for the weapon he would kill her with. No knives or guns. No curvy daggers. Maybe his hands. Would he strangle her?

"I'm not going to kill you," he said, eyes tearing up. "Not me… But I'm definitely responsible."

"You don't have to do this," she said. "Just let me go. I'll leave town and I won't ever come back. You can say you did it and no one will ever know the truth."

He rubbed his brow. "Maybe so, but I'll know… And so will *it.*"

Chapter 23

The driver's door slammed. Mr. Valcourt slumped down, holding a half-glass of that magical elixir that was slowly putting him to sleep and loosening his tongue. Becca yanked on the door handle, releasing the door.

Mr. Valcourt stumbled forward to stop her, but he tripped on his own big feet. Becca herself fell out the door just as the driver caught her by the arm.

"Stop her!" shouted Mr. Valcourt.

She was stopped. The driver was very strong. His fingers dug into her. "Where do you want her?"

"Let me go!" she screamed.

Straightening his jacket, Mr. Valcourt exited the limo. "Nowhere yet. We're gonna need to tie her up."

"No!" She thrashed and fought. She stamped her heel

down on the driver's foot. The only damage she managed was a scuff to his polished shoe.

Mr. Valcourt and the driver dragged her around to the back of the limo, and then they switched — Mr. Valcourt held onto her while the driver fished out his key and unlocked the trunk. She fought harder, yet somehow the older man was much stronger than she would have guessed,

I'm not going in there! No!

All that was inside was a spare tire, a roadside safety kit, and a pile of rope. Lots of rope.

"Did you hear that?" asked Mr. Valcourt.

"What?" asked the driver.

Mr. Valcourt shushed them. They froze and listened, even Becca, whose heart pounded so loudly that she couldn't hear anything other than their voices.

Whatever Mr. Valcourt thought he heard, no one else picked up on it.

"I don't know…" he said after a while. "I thought I heard another car."

"Or maybe it was—"

Mr. Valcourt glared at him. "No, not yet. Now help me out."

They yanked Becca's arms behind her back, and when she fought against that too, Mr. Valcourt kicked her legs out from under her body. She dropped to her knees; the impact vibrated throughout her skeletal system. Even her teeth chattered together.

Working quickly, they wrapped the rope around her

wrists, binding her snuggly. Then they worked on her ankles. Neither noticed the garden snips tucked into her shoe; the tool had slipped under her foot, making her arch bulge and strain against the canvas sneakers.

She squirmed on the dirt, trying to get to her feet when the driver bent down, picked her up, and threw her over his shoulder.

"No!" she cried. "You can't do this!"

She argued and shouted and screamed. No one was around to hear her, and her pleas were for naught.

They carried her to the grain elevator and around to a narrow door. It had been padlocked, and for a fleeting moment, Becca thought they would have to turn around and go home. Maybe it was all a prank. *A Harvest Festival prank. They pull this on all the queens. Yeah!*

Four women had been killed.

This was no prank.

Mr. Valcourt reached into his breast pocket and pulled out a small blue box. It was coated in velvet and appeared to be something one would give to a significant other who would be delighted to find pearl earrings or a diamond bracelet. When he popped it open, there was a key inside.

Becca's breath hitched.

The key fit the padlock. Mr. Valcourt unlocked it and dragged the thick chain through slowly, careful not to rattle it too much. Then he pushed the door open. "Let's make this quick," he whispered.

As soon as they entered, something rustled around at their feet. Critters and leaves scattered in all directions.

Every crackle and scuttle sent chills down Becca's spine.

"I don't want to be here," she said.

"Me neither," the driver muttered.

"Shut up!" Mr. Valcourt snapped. "Don't make any sudden moves or sounds, for Christ's sake."

Inside the grain elevator, a few weathered boards had long ago dried up and fallen off the higher levels of the building, creating a rough skylight.

Becca saw stars twinkling above. But, any kind of narrow gap that she could possibly escape through on the ground level had been boarded up. There was no easy way out.

Mr. Valcourt walked into the center of the space. His shoes scraped over what little grain remained on the ground. A few small mice raced by. He lifted a foot to avoid them, and finally just pointed to a random spot.

"I don't care. Drop her anywhere, so we can get the hell out of here," he said.

"Good," said the driver. "This place gives me the creeps."

He set Becca down where Mr. Valcourt indicated and made a beeline for the door. He didn't even bother to wait.

A mouse scurried too close to Becca and she yelped. Mr. Valcourt squatted down next to her. He was reaching into his jacket again. She expected another mysteriously beautiful box, but this time it was anything but. He had a rusty box cutter.

She stared as he pushed the blade out.

"You think I was going to use my fine cutlery for this?

Ha, yeah, right. It doesn't care."

"Please, don't..."

"Here's the thing," he said. "In about five minutes, none of this is going to matter. No one's going to remember you. Just like no one remembers the others."

"I remember them!" Becca said, stretching toward him. "My mom and—"

"Yeah, but I bet you don't know their names."

"—and Millie Sawyer and—"

"Their names are not important. What's important is that we do this. You're now a part of something incredible. You're going to save our town. Your mother was supposed to do it in 1966, but that insufferable bitch knew something was up and thought getting knocked up would stop things. Obviously not, but she tainted the tradition. Our ... our guest likes things pure. So when your slut mom spread her legs for that idiot Paul Leblanc, she really screwed over our town."

Becca squeezed her eyes shut and tried to focus on the women before her. "Marsha McCreedy and—"

"We don't know what it is or why it's here — it's just always been here," continued Mr. Valcourt. "Attempts to ... eradicate it have been unsuccessful. All we know is that if we feed it, Morganville prospers. I'm not going to argue with history."

"—Viola Pettit and Bethany St. James—"

"You can stop that now," he said. "It's not going to do any good."

"Dorothy St. James!"

He grabbed a handful of her hair and jerked her head back, stretching her neck until she feared it would snap. He shook her, forcing her to open her eyes and look into the darkness.

Something moved in the shadows.

But how could there be shadows at night?

A shape, like a man, moved back and forth. It paced like a tiger, preparing to hunt.

Hunting.

Becca shivered. She couldn't focus on what she was seeing — or not seeing — but she heard a low, guttural growl. A snort. It was watching her.

"Isn't that something," Mr. Valcourt breathed into her ear. "It's been with us for as long as the town has existed. Maybe longer than that. No one knows, and no one will ever know. We can only feed it and get on with our lives."

"P-please—"

"There's only one thing left for you to do."

He swiped the box cutter across her collarbone and down her chest. Not too deep, but enough to sting and draw blood. She gasped. He pulled her hair even harder, ripping at her scalp.

"Now scream, queen!" he hissed, shoving her to the ground.

He dashed to the door and slammed it shut behind him. Safe on the other side, he fumbled with the chain and padlock. The driver made a comment about the lock and Mr. Valcourt snapped at him. "I don't want *either* of them to get out!"

Becca braced herself for a sudden attack, but the creature remained in the darkness, stalking her. After a few moments, the only thing she heard was the limo's motor as the two men drove away. She began to wonder if she had only imagined seeing something.

Maybe there was nothing at all.

And then it moved. One clawed, blackened foot stepped out of the darkness.

She arched her back, reaching her bound hands toward her sneaker. Twisting her ankle, she pressed the heel of her shoe against the ground and pried it off her foot. Instant relief for her instep, but the snips were caught in the shoe. She stretched further, pulling several muscles.

The creature stepped another foot out. It rose up high on its haunches. The only light was the twinkle of the lights and sliver of the moon in the broken skylight above.

The thing — man or beast, she couldn't tell — was large and hairy. Or was it a viscous, shifting bag of fluid? Or was it a charred body of a human? It was too dark to be certain of anything.

The sight of it froze Becca in place.

Move! she screamed at herself — but she refused to scream for Mr. Valcourt or this awful town. If she had to bite off her own tongue, she wouldn't scream.

The creature didn't seem capable of seeing her properly. Its head jerked back and forth. Tipping its gnarled face up toward the sky, it sniffed the air. Then it snapped to attention and dashed toward her.

Becca flinched and turned away, just as her fingers

curled around the handle of the snips. She flicked off the safety and the two sharp blades sprang apart.

Holding back a sigh, she began to very quietly, very softly *clip, clip, clip* at the rope around her ankles. The fibers frayed and split, and then her legs were free. But she couldn't run away yet. Her wrists were still bound together, and the creature loomed over her.

It smacked its lips, tasting blood in the air.

Please, please, please go away.

That wasn't going to happen. Whatever this thing was, it was here for her.

It smacked its head against her shoulder, forcing her onto her back. Her hand slipped. The snips caught under her body and cut into her palm. She fought to stay curled in a ball, but the creature slammed against her again and again. Each time, the snips carved into her hand.

Stepping on her dress, the creature leaned in close. Hot, drool salivated down its face and globbed on Becca's stomach, chest, and shoulders. It got down on all fours and began to sniff her from crotch to neck. When it got to her throat, it rumbled against her skin and darted back down to her chest.

Its tongue slid out of its mouth and traced her wound. Becca's chest stung as its prickly tongue prodded her flesh, lapping up the blood.

She couldn't wait any longer. She arched her back and slid the snips across her hand until they were embedded in the rope. Then she cut and cut, trying not to move any other part of her body.

The rope gave away. Becca squeezed her arm out, gripping her only weapon. The creature reeled back just in time to see what she held. It screeched, revealing rows and rows of sharp, little teeth embedded in its mouth, going far down, deep into its throat. Becca shrieked and stabbed the snips into its neck. She released the safety notch and the snips opened wide.

Howling, the creature fell backward. It clawed at its neck as Becca scrambled for the door. She threw herself against the only exit, but the padlock held. She pushed. There was just enough room to squeeze herself through. It was a tight fit, but she could just make it.

The creature roared, yanking the snips out.

Becca shoved one leg out. Then her head and chest, smearing blood on the door. She had to crouch down low to fit under the chain — and got stuck. She clawed at the grass, rocks, anything for leverage.

She was almost out when the creature bashed against the door. It gave her an extra inch to squeeze through, but at the last second, the creature snared her leg.

Its claws dug in, ripping her flesh from calf to ankle and tearing off her remaining shoe. This time she scream-ed. She couldn't help it. The creature was shredding her.

She tumbled away, leaving blood and skin behind, and hobbled down to where the limo had been. It was long gone now, but she followed the tracks.

Behind her, the creature howled. It frantically threw its body against the sides of the building until the wooden walls cracked and split open, releasing it into the night.

Chapter 24

"There has to be something *we can do.*"

"*There's not.*"

Becca's voice played on a loop inside James's head, making him angrier and angrier. The finality of her words frustrated him.

He kept prodding her to think through the problem with him, but she had given up.

He couldn't just leave her to fend for herself.

So after he dropped her at home early that Saturday morning, he said goodbye and watched her go inside. Then he drove off, but instead of going home, he circled the block and parked down the street from her house. He waited all morning and into the afternoon, nodding off in the driver's seat. He opened a warm can of Diet Coke his mom kept in the glovebox and hoped the caffeine would keep him awake.

Later that afternoon, Declan Valcourt and a contingent of other people (a few James knew from school, Travis among them, of course) arrived at Becca's house. That woke him up. Their presence meant something was about to go down.

They lingered in the house for a few hours, long enough for James to feel sluggish again — and then a limo arrived. Everyone exited the house. A bossy lady in a pants suit took photos, and soon after Valcourt and Becca disappeared into the limo.

James followed them.

It was after sundown at this point, but he maintained a safe distance, headlights off. The limo turned down a rocky road and toward a grain elevator. But James never got close enough to see it because a black car peeled out in front of him and blocked his path.

He slammed on his brakes at the last second, skidding through the dirt road. He held his breath, bracing for impact, but before they could collide, the station wagon came to a halt.

His gaze traveled down the length of the car's hood until he looked in the eyes of the other driver.

Travis fucking Valcourt.

Travis jumped out of the idling Pontiac wearing a fucking tuxedo like it was prom night. He ran over to the station wagon and threw open the door, grabbing a fistful of James's shirt and dragging him out.

Before hitting the ground, James took a hit from

Travis. His teeth rattled in their sockets and the impact knocked the glasses off his face. They landed somewhere in the dirt. James tried to kick them under the car so they wouldn't get stomped on.

"Come here, you piece of shit." Travis hauled him up on his feet and punched him in the lower ribs. James coughed. Something cracked. Travis shoved him up against the car and laid into him with another punch. "Whaddaya think you're doin'? You wanna fuck up our town? Well, no fuckin' way!"

Travis punched him over and over again. James's face was still tender and bruised from the last beating he took, so he couldn't tell if Travis hit harder than the other guys or if they had just softened him up for this second assault.

He lost count of how many times Travis belted him when he blacked out. He came to laying on the ground.

Travis kicked him in the gut with his pointed-toe dress shoes. James hacked up blood. When Travis paused for a second to start a long-winded speech about "Becca's civic duty," James sucked up all his bloody spit and shot it at Travis's leg. The congealed glob sludged down his perfectly creased pants and collected on his shoe.

That shut him up.

James gave him a deranged, bloody-toothed grin. Travis wound up for another kick as James punched him in the balls. Travis doubled over. James grabbed him by his lapels and dragged him down into the dirt.

"I'm gonna fucking kill you!" Travis roared.

The two rolled around in the grass and mud, trading

hits. James took the brunt of the hits, but finally plowed his fist into Travis's perfect nose. The cartilage cracked under his knuckles. Blood erupted and flowed down Travis's lips and chin, spilling onto his white shirt.

"Fuck!" he spat, rolling off.

James hit him again. Travis scurried away, holding a hand under his nose as if to collect his own precious blood. Adrenaline pumping, James chased Travis back to his Firebird. Travis slammed the door in his face just in time. James slapped a bloody hand against the window.

"Where's Becca?!" James shrieked.

"Get the fuck away from me, freak!"

"Tell me!"

"Fuck you!" Travis put the car in reverse, steering wildly to escape James's fury.

James jumped out of the way, narrowly avoiding a hit. Left in the dust, he stumbled onto the ground, finding his glasses. Even though a sharp pain stabbed him every time he tried to take a deep breath, James figured he won.

Holding his side, James stumbled back to the car. As soon as he got behind the wheel, he put on his glasses and flicked on the lights.

Limping toward him in a bloodied white gown was Becca.

* * *

Becca staggered down the rocky path, dragging her leg behind her. Her lungs burned and her leg screamed.

Fearing what she might see, she didn't dare look at it — she stayed focused on the road ahead. In the distance, she heard voices. Yelling. She slowed down. A car engine fired up. She feared another encounter with Mr. Valcourt, but she couldn't stop. The creature was close behind.

Headlights flashed on, blinding her. She held up a hand to shield her eyes.

Mrs. Martin's station wagon was parked crookedly in the middle of the road. Had she not been a throbbing, bleeding mess, Becca would have been furious that James didn't listen to her. Instead, she felt relieved that he had come to her rescue, even though he would soon be dead meat.

We'll be dead meat together.

She waved her arms in the air as she raced toward him. A mixture of tears and sweat blurred her vision, but all she had to do was head toward the light.

"James!" she cried.

He stepped out of the car, holding his side. He shuffled toward her.

"No! Stay in the car!"

This time he listened, getting back inside.

When she was close enough to open the passenger side door, she stole a look back the way she had come.

There was nothing but blackness.

That didn't mean the creature wasn't hiding in the shadows.

She dove in and locked the door. "Dri—"

Just as she turned and saw James's bloody, bashed-in

face, a huge black shape covered the windshield. *Crack!* Spiderwebs of broken glass spread out as the creature pressed its form against the car. It drew back its arm to strike. James shifted the car into reverse and slammed on the gas. The car shot backwards.

The creature tried to hold on for dear life, but James's wild steering shook it off the hood. Then he reversed, turning on the narrow road until they were headed in the direction of the town. He hit the gas again and they were off.

But before they could get too far down the road, Becca grabbed his wrist.

"I have an idea."

Chapter 25

*D*eclan Valcourt was three sheets to the wind when an unfamiliar station wagon pulled up in his driveway. He poured himself another scotch, wondering if his idiot son drank too much at the festival and needed one of his loser friends to drive his sorry ass home. Not that Mr. Valcourt would give him hell for it. Not tonight.

Tonight was ... not easy.

Maybe not for those poor unsuspecting bastards, he thought. Everyone in town could live it up and enjoy the festivities, but heavy is the head that wears the crown.

He shuffled out of his office just as the unexpected guest pounded on the door.

What the hell is this? he wondered. *Everyone should be at the goddamn festival.*

That's where he was supposed to be. He was supposed to cut the ribbon on some new construction project, and shake hands with some bigwig toting a bag full of cash, but he just couldn't face those people. Not tonight.

The elder members on the council had told him tonight would be difficult. They remembered the '67 festival. They remembered Bethany St. James and her squealing infant. "It wasn't pleasant," was all they said. *When is human sacrifice ever pleasant?* he wondered. But he did not think he would feel this conflicted.

His stomach lurched when he saw Becca St. James on his doorstep. His drunk fingers released his glass. It shattered across the floor, and the sight of the bloodied, pissed-off girl just about broke him too.

She can't be here. She can't be HERE.

"What're you—? You can't— *You have to go."*

"No!" she shouted. Her shrill voice startled him and she pushed her way in.

He pointed to the door. *"Get out."*

"Fuck you!"

He backed away. She didn't have a weapon, and so he figured if he could get to his office, he could find the boxcutter.

That thing out there would just have to be satisfied with a cold meal. *Speaking of which...* "Where is it?"

She took another step, leaving a bloody footprint in her wake. Her leg had been torn to shreds. He didn't know how she was able to stand, and then before she could answer his question, she took three quick steps and fell against him. He stumbled backwards against a small decorative table, knocking over a vase.

They stared into each other's eyes as Becca wiped a hand across her bleeding, oozing chest and collected a palmful of blood. Then she smeared it across his forehead.

He pushed her to the floor. "Get the fuck out of my house!"

She tried to stand, but slipped on her own mess. The coppery scent mixed with the taste of scotch in his mouth, making his gut churn. *Ugh...*

At the end of the driveway, something big and deadly howled.

Mr. Valcourt got down on one knee and picked Becca up by the straps of her dress. He shook her like a ragdoll. Her heavy eyelids fluttered as she laughed. He slapped her. *"Do you realize what you've done?!"*

He dropped her and ran to his office. She crawled after him, but he slammed the door on her and locked it. With a whimper, she scratched and pawed at the door.

The creature howled again. It was closer this time.

From the safety of his office, Mr. Valcourt listened as Becca padded away, climbed the stairs, and ran across the hallway. One of the doors upstairs slammed. He could even hear the click of the tiny lock on the bathroom door. *Stupid bitch*, he thought. *That'll never hold.* The creature would track her down, bust in, and tear her apart.

At least she would be dead and this would all be over. For the next twenty years at least.

By then, Mr. Valcourt would make sure to take all his

earnings from over the years and invest in a secret over-
seas bank account. He would be long gone before this
stinking town would need to host another goddamn
Harvest Festival.

Upstairs, the shower turned on.

What the fuck *is she doing?* He gripped the doorknob,
about to charge up after her and throw her bleeding ass
out on the street. *Make her fulfill her civic duty, just like
I have to.* But he paused when he heard footsteps.
Someone — or something — had entered the house.
Claws scratched the floor.

The thing was inside.

God-fucking-damn it!

It sniffed and snorted across the foyer to Mr. Valcourt's office. He could see its shadow across the bottom
of the door. It tapped its big toe, clacking its yellowed,
talon-like nail on the floor. *Tap, tap, tap.*

It suddenly slammed its bulk against the door. Mr.
Valcourt let out a yelp, jumping backward and crashing
against one of his sofas, which skidded against a side table
and knocked over a pile of books. *Christ!*

The creature knew he was inside. It began clawing at
the door, rattling the doorknob. The wood on the other
side began to splinter and crack. Mr. Valcourt thought he
had paid good money for this house and goddamn it if
those lazy, son of bitch contractors didn't install the finest,
heaviest doors. *If I get out of this, I'm going to sue!*

If? No, WHEN.

The door burst apart. Chunks of wood splintered

everywhere. The creature leered at him, turning its head from side to side before tearing its way through the rest of the door.

Mr. Valcourt ran around his desk to the window. He never opened this window. Not even to get fresh air. Who needed fresh air when he had paid a pretty penny for central air conditioning?

Mr. Valcourt had done really well for himself and his family, considering the rest of the town had been circling the drain for a number of years.

All because that bitch Beth St. James couldn't just shut the fuck up and do her part.

But Mr. Valcourt would do his part.

He turned around. The creature had dismantled the door. It shuffled into the room and snapped its jaws. Spit flung across the fine furnishings.

Mr. Valcourt rubbed his face. *Fuck, the blood. That fucking cunt's blood is on me.* He scrubbed his face as hard as he could using the crook of his elbow, then pointed upstairs toward the sound of the running shower. "She's upstairs. The girl with the big, bloody cut on her chest? *She's* the one you want."

The creature growled, closing in. Why couldn't it understand just a few simple words?

Maybe because we've kept it locked up in that grain elevator decade after decade and never really bothered to try communicating with it, just using it as our own little piggy bank to crack open in emergencies.

Mr. Valcourt shook away that intrusive thought. It

wasn't his problem to fix; it was someone else's to inherit.

"Upstairs!" He kept pointing and talking louder. *"She's upstairs!"*

The creature cocked its head, sizing him up. They were only a desk-length apart. Still sniffing, the creature turned.

Mr. Valcourt sighed. *Finally.* "Fucking idiot," he muttered.

The creature spun around and with Mr. Valcourt just beginning to lower his arm back down, the creature reached out and tore it clean off. Blood sprayed everywhere. It scrambled over the desk and jumped on top of the reeve, screaming bloody murder.

The last thing Mr. Valcourt ever saw were rows of impossibly sharp teeth closing in on his horrified face.

* * *

Becca left the shower running and grabbed a towel. One of those perfectly white, plush towels that only hotels and rich people seemed to have a never-ending supply of. She wrapped it around herself, holding it tightly to her cut chest. Blood continued to seep out, so she looted the medicine cabinet for a box of oversized bandages and stuck two on herself. Maybe it would slow the bleeding enough to prevent the creature from sniffing her out — but her leg was still torn to hell and she needed a lot more than fancy towels to stop the bleeding.

From the medicine cabinet, she grabbed a pair of

cuticle scissors.

Trapped in the house, she listened to Mr. Valcourt's screams. The odds were that only one of the two monsters would survive, and she would have to confront the victor.

Neither one was going to let her get out alive.

Because the creature went after Mr. Valcourt first, she had time to set her trap. Gripping the scissors, Becca hid in the linen closet and held her breath.

Once Mr. Valcourt stopped making sounds, the creature rustled around on the main floor, until it picked up her scent. It raced up the stairs, banging against the railing and knocking photos off the wall until it sniffed its way to the bathroom. It howled.

I'm coming for you.

Just as it had to Mr. Valcourt's office, the creature made short work of the door.

Through the closet door slats, Becca watched the creature break in. It sniffed around the laundry hamper and followed her bloody mess to the shower.

Becca held her breath and tried to be brave. She thought about James, waiting outside. "I just need enough time to trap the thing," she told him.

"I'll give you five minutes and then I'm coming after you."

"Ten." He was about to argue when she cut him off. "This thing is after *me*. Not you. You're safe as long as you stay out of the way. Please, just ten minutes and then we'll go wherever you want."

He gave in. But if he hadn't, Becca would have had to

punch his lights out.

Inside the bathroom, the creature paused at the linen closet. Becca braced herself for its claws to tear through the slats and rip her heart out. But it passed her by, continuing toward the shower curtain, where it dropped down to inhale the bloodied bathmat and the wet clump of her dress.

Blood trickled from her leg wound, pooling at her heel. She couldn't wait any longer. She opened the closet door.

The creature leapt up, snarling. Becca gasped as it attacked the shower curtain. It moved so brutally fast that she had only a few seconds before it realized no one was there.

Throwing one arm around the creature's neck, she jammed the scissors into its throat. The creature shrieked and thrashed about. It bashed Becca against the counter and then hurled her against the towel rack, where she struck the back of her head.

Tossing her aside, the creature whipped around and attacked. Becca stumbled on her gimpy leg, missing its claws, which busted the mirror. Shards of glass shattered, embedding in its hand. It yowled.

Becca launched at the creature. *One more time!* She reached up and twisted the scissors like a corkscrew, just as the creature reared back. The scissors popped out. Blood spurted everywhere. The creature wrestled her to the ground as she dashed for the door. Her chin hit the tiles, teeth gnashing together.

As the creature dragged her away from her only

escape, Becca rolled onto her side and shoved the scissors up and under its chin. The sharp blades cut through its tongue and speared the roof of its mouth. Blood leaked everywhere as it howled. Becca withdrew the scissors and stabbed again. And again. And again…

The creature tried to get away, pulling itself down the hall. Becca crawled after it, continuing to stab and gouge the creature until it bled out and stopped moving.

Then she collapsed against the wall next to it. She nudged the body with her foot. It was dead. Opening her palm, she let the scissors drop to the floor.

It was over.

With a shuddering sigh, she burst into tears.

Long live the queen.

After

*B*ecca stared at the words scratched into the side of her hatchback. It was bad enough the little gray car had rust around the wheel wells and cracks in the windshield. It was all she could afford when she moved to the city. Now some bitter neighbor used the time she spent packing up Gran's house to make their feelings known.

DIE BITCH!

She traced a thumb over the letters. One last goodbye from Morganville, she figured.

She couldn't be too mad about it. After all, she was able to leave this miserable town. After what transpired, no one wanted her there. So she took her meager savings, found a small apartment near the university, and got a job waitressing while she finished her final year of studies through a distance learning program.

Even with several arduous weeks in rehab for her leg, she still managed to finish her final exam before James finished his. And she was riding high on the excitement of receiving her diploma one week before Christmas when she decided to return to town one last time.

James had stayed behind to help his mom. Mrs. Martin refused to leave even after her client base dried up. She dug her heels in and tried to make it work. James couldn't bear to leave her, so he found a job in St. Aubergine and commuted back and forth each day. He finished the rest of his courses through a small satellite education center near his work.

Neither he nor Becca could continue classes at Morganville High. Not after what happened the night of the Harvest Festival.

After killing the creature in the Valcourt house, Becca limped downstairs to find the reeve sprawled out in the foyer. Either he crawled to the door in an attempt to flee the house or the creature had left him this way, like a half-eaten snack. His eyes had been scratched out of his face, yet he was somehow still alive, though not for much longer.

His head jerked from side to side as she neared him. "Who's there?"

"Who do you think?" she growled.

When he started gagging, she rolled him onto his side. He spat up globs of gore, his eviscerated insides slopping onto his luxurious flooring.

"It's the town," he sputtered, as she knelt beside him. "You feed it, you feed the town… You kill it, you kill the town."

Fuck the town, she thought, collapsing next to him.

James found her shortly after. He had stuck by his promise.

When Travis and his mom returned later that night, Mrs. Valcourt just screamed and cried and yanked out her hair, while Travis stared at his father's corpse. His unconscious ex-girlfriend laid in James's arms.

When the RCMP officers and EMTs arrived, James hitched a ride in Becca's ambulance. He held her hand the entire way, telling her what a stupid, crazy thing she had done.

"It's over," she said, before passing out again.

Months later, with her diploma framed on her wall and Gran's house up for sale, Becca knew it wasn't over. Her new life was just beginning.

Ignoring the scratches on her car, Becca threw her suitcases and a box of her mom's and Gran's possessions into the backseat. As she pulled away from the house, she glanced at the "for sale" sign. It wasn't the only one on the block; four other neighbors had also decided to pull up stakes.

Becca drove to James's house. He waited at the front door with a backpack slung over his shoulder and a bulky duffle bag stuffed with clothes and books at his feet. He smiled as he ran to the car. His mom waved from behind the screen door, and then disappeared inside.

He leaned in through the driver's side window and kissed Becca. She touched his face, healed after Travis's beatdown, aside from a broken nose that left a small bump. His new glasses hid it nicely.

"Where's you mom?" Becca asked. "I thought she wanted to see the apartment?"

"She really wants to make a go of this place," he said, cramming his bags into the back. "Said she can't be seen with us. You know…"

She nodded. "We're bad for business."

"Exactly."

He hurried back around the car and got in the passenger side. If he noticed the *DIE BITCH*, he didn't mention it. Not yet. Instead, he turned her face toward him and gave her a long, sweet kiss. She ached for more when they parted.

In the last few weeks, they had been so busy packing and figuring out moving details that they had spent very little time together.

"We'd better get driving," he said.

She took the shortest route out of town — without having to pass the grain elevator. They still had to drive by the library, the sight of which made Becca tear up. She knew there were bigger, better libraries in the city and even within the university she had applied to, but there was just something about having a local branch that just felt homey.

They cut across main street and headed for the underpass, and that's when Becca saw Travis. He carried a stack of flyers with Heath and Chester in tow. They trailed behind, laughing and pushing each other around. Meanwhile, Travis had a cold, stony look on his face.

He hadn't been the same since his dad died.

He wore a black armband around his puffy ski jacket and was diligently posting flyers on every telephone poll and community board. A few shops even allowed him to put some in their windows.

VOTE TRAVIS VALCOURT FOR TOWN COUNCIL
– SPRING 1985

Becca shivered.

"Cold?" James asked, reaching to turn up the heat.

"Yeah," she said.

The blast of hot, stuffy air didn't help. It wasn't the subzero temperature that disturbed her; it was that Travis hadn't learned from the past.

After Becca had been discharged from the hospital, Travis came to see her. A horrible grimace was carved into his grief-stricken face. He must have lost ten or twenty pounds. He cried and punched a wall during their conversation, but Becca remained calm with her hands folded in her lap. James and Mrs. Martin sat in the kitchen, ready to intervene if Travis tried to attack her.

He begged her to tell him what happened to his father. He wanted the truth, not the watered-down version the other council members and the police gave him. So Becca told him. She even showed him her notes, and explained what the town had been using the festival for. What it had done to all those women. She calmly laid out exactly how she had escaped from a horrid, unexplainable creature in the grain elevator and how she led it to his father — though she omitted having done so on purpose.

He saw right through her.

"Fucking bitch," he spat before storming off and slamming the door.

Nobody knew what happened to the creature. Despite repeatedly calling the RCMP, Becca and James never received a straight answer. One officer said the body had been cremated and disposed of. Another said he would have to follow up with them, and then didn't.

Becca and James even tried returning to the grain elevator to check, but were startled away by sounds in the surrounding woods. She hyperventilated in the backseat, her chest wound seeping, as James sped away from the site. She hadn't been able to force herself to go back.

As they passed Travis on the street, she thought about waving, but that seemed glib. Instead she waited until she caught his eye and nodded. He scowled, flyers fluttering against his chest. He held up a gloved hand and gave her the finger.

You're not going to win with that attitude, she thought.

Before they drove through the underpass and merged onto the highway, they passed the last few shops on main street. Most had a foreclosed or for lease sign in the window. Even the burger joint was closing up shop. Soon there would be nothing left. The whole town would blow away, like the wisps of a dandelion.

Unless Travis could save it. Maybe it was possible, but she hoped not.

Not if another girl's life depended on it.

Staring down the highway, Becca held James's hand and imagined a bigger and better life to come.

The End

Thank you for reading!

Being an indie author is hard work, so I thank you for finding and reading my book. If you enjoyed it, please leave a review or tell a friend. Or review a friend and tell me about them. I like judging people.

— *S.S.*

About the Author

Retro horror author Stephanie Sparks writes stories reminiscent of classic 70s and 80s slasher and monster movies. She loves scream queens, final girls, and the masked maniacs who stalk them. Her books feature action, thrills, dark humour, and sarcasm. She prefers cats to people, and when she's not lost in a paperback from hell or listening to 1980s movie soundtracks, she's day-dreaming ideas for her next book or writing furiously.

See what she's working on at StephanieSparks.ca.

Also Available

Kill the Babysitter

Jane's first babysitting gig comes with a lot of rules, and after a hellish night, she breaks an important one: *Don't let the kids play with the Ouija board.* Now the mischievous spirit in the board wants to play a deadly new game: *Kill the Babysitter.* Jane must fight tooth and nail against a murderous horde of possessed children — and if she doesn't team up with her worst enemy, she may not survive the night.

The Stepchildren

Jamie had always suspected something was wrong with her stepfather. Burt wasn't just a man on the hunt for the perfect life — he was a fugitive family annihilator. Years after surviving his attack, Jamie and his other stepchildren come together in group therapy where they learn he has died in prison. Or has he? Turns out, even in death, stepdaddy dearest has a few deadly surprises left for his wayward stepchildren.

See more at StephanieSparks.ca.

Preview

KILL THE BABYSITTER

Available now

March 2019

Jane Freeman was washing paint brushes in the sink when the Beast attacked her in broad daylight. Six feet of puffy, ruddy skin and brown eyes that simmered with hatred, the Beast wanted her dead from day one.

Everyone has had that one bully that scared the living daylights of them, that forced you to fake a sick day or beg your parents to homeschool you. But by the time you reach adulthood, the memories of those horrid people mostly fade away — or send you to therapy or the bottle. In the moment, all you can do is try to survive.

The Beast stalked the halls of Morganville High looking for trouble. Looking for Jane. Tall, wide, and menacing, the Beast was built like a rugby player. In just the few months she had been attending Jane's school, the Beast had made Jane's life a living hell. Jane had no idea what she had done to incur the much bigger, stronger girl's wrath, but sometimes it didn't matter who you were. Anyone could get caught in the grinding wheel of high school.

That wheel had ground Jane down enough for several lifetimes. Her parents had divorced, and she hadn't seen her dad in years; her mom worked long, late nights at the hospital in town. She was a C-student with a paper due every damn week. And she was seventeen without a car, forced to take the bus to school and her feet everywhere else.

All she could do was fantasize about her dream car, a hot blue Mustang with black leather seats. Then she would be free, driving across the U.S. to retrace the old Route 66. And then she could finally have some fun.

Until then, she had to endure the Beast, and up until that Tuesday afternoon, she had been doing very well at avoiding her. They only shared two classes a week: Miss Smithers' chill-as-fuck art hour.

Maybe things had been going too well in the class. Jane was getting Bs (Miss Smithers handed 'em out like candy if her students simply applied themselves) and arguing less with the popular kids about the music they played. (Emily Burke and Brad Polanski and their goons swarmed the big table by the stereo so they could control the music, and they played Drake's droning, monotonous bullshit every chance they got, and then they shat over

Jane's suggestions to play Ozzy and Led Zeppelin.)

So that Tuesday morning, when it was Jane's turn to wash the brushes at the end of class, she mindlessly hummed one of the less annoying Drake songs. A heavy set of hands slammed against her back — the Beast's paws! Turning to see, Jane knocked her hip against the counter.

"Ow!" she yelped

The Beast's puffy, red face was too close. Her hot, post-lunch breath blew into Jane's face. *"Leave me alone,"* she growled, before shoving Jane again.

Jane fell against the sink. The other students screeched back in their chairs, ooh-ing excitedly as they gathered around. The phones they weren't supposed to have in class came out in droves, clutched in trembling hands as a hush fell over the room. Everyone understood this wasn't the time for wisecracks.

It was time for a fight.

Jane gripped the brushes, watching the Beast stomp away. Her hip throbbed and her back itched where the Beast slammed into her. Her ego raged red-hot.

Without a second to think, she threw the brushes at the Beast's back. The Beast spun around, teeth gritted.

Jane turned to flee. Her sneakered foot landed on one of the brushes, and she skidded, falling face first onto the popular kids' table. Emily leaned in with her camera as Jane almost crashed into her.

"Extreme close-up," cracked a cute brown-haired boy. Nate-something. His blue eyes shined as he flashed her a grin. He only registered in Jane's world because her friend Lily wouldn't stop gushing about him.

"What is going on in here?!" cried Miss Smithers as Jane picked herself up.

The Beast fled the room.

After the conflict simmered down, the principal and Miss Smithers sent Jane to the nurse's office. She laid on a cot in the dimly lit nurse's office, holding a bag of ice against her hip, jeans pulled down low. The nurse asked her a million questions that her mom would probably ask when she got home. Eventually the nurse had to slip out to deal with another student and Jane got to lay back and stare at the ceiling.

She wondered what they were doing to the Beast. The girl was probably being yelled at by Principal Hector. Then she would be suspended, maybe even expelled. The school had a "no tolerance" policy for bullying and fighting — but that was only if the *school* determined it was bullying.

Regardless, Jane couldn't help but smile, imagining being free of that horrible girl for the rest of the year.

After about an hour of lounging around, Jane had company. The nurse shuffled in with the cute boy from art class. Nate. He sat down on the opposite cot and smiled shyly, trying not to notice that Jane's jeans were pulled down, exposing her bony, bruised hip. She didn't feel very voluptuous, but the blush that crept up his face made her feel self-conscious.

As soon as the nurse was gone, she sat up and adjusted

her clothes. "Hey," she said.

"Hey," he said right back.

"What're you in for?"

He grinned and rolled up his pant leg. "Sprained ankle."

It didn't look swollen or hurt in any way. It looked like a teenage boy's hairy, skinny ankle. "Uh, what?"

The nurse poked her head back into the room. Age had etched deep, angry lines into her dour face. "No talking."

Both students nodded and waited until she was gone. Then Nate took a seat on her rolling stool and cruised closer to Jane. Keeping his voice low, he said, "I just wanted to see the girl who slayed the Beast."

Slayed? Jane had replayed the fight over and over as she sat in purgatory. All she had done was throw brushes at the girl. She didn't commit murder. "What're you talking about?"

"The Beast is gone," he said. "The principal keeps calling her to the office. Haven't you heard?"

Jane had not. The nurse's office was the only room in the building that didn't have a speaker for the PA system. All she heard was muffled announcements from the hallway.

But she didn't believe the Beast was gone. More like "escaped." The Beast was loose.

She swallowed, thoughts flying through her mind at a mile a minute. "I need a car," she muttered.

She had needed a car since the Beast first started intimidating her. Following her home from school on a few occasions. When she tried taking the bus, the Beast would be there too. But a car was the ultimate safe space. The Beast couldn't get her then.

"I could give you a ride..."

She looked up. A ride was currency, but it was also used to barter. Cash, grass, or ass — nobody rides for free. She gave him a side-eyed look, summoning her usual bravado. "Sorry. I don't take rides from strangers."

"Even if I have candy?" he said with that damned grin.

Jane couldn't help it. She grinned back, running a hand through her messy, black curls. *No wonder Lily likes this guy. He's kinda cute.* "What's your name?" she asked, as if she didn't know.

"Nate Crawford," he said. Then he did something weird — he reached out to shake her hand. She let him, but no one had ever done that before. His skin was warm and dry, and he held her just long enough to make her blush. When he let go, she almost floated off the cot. "I'm pretty new here. Just moved last month. And you're Jane Freeman."

"Yeah. How'd you know that?"

He shrugged. "I've seen you around."

"Oh," was all she could say. "Cool."

"About that ride? I can't take you very far. Also promised a friend I'd drive him to yoga. But if you don't trust me — *yet* — bring a friend. I'll get you outta here safe and sound. It could be fun."

Stroking her chin, she pretended to mull it over. "Yeah, okay. I could use some fun."

Want more?

Order your copy today:

Amazon
Barnes & Noble
Blackwell's
Booktopia
Kobo
Waterstones
And more…